THE SECRET
OF SKYTOP HILL
and Other Stories

THE SECRET OF SKYTOP HILL
and Other Stories

by
ENID BLYTON

Illustrated by
Pythia Ashton-Jewell

AWARD PUBLICATIONS LIMITED

For further information on Enid Blyton please visit *www.blyton.com*

ISBN 978-1-84135-495-8

This edition entitled *The Secret of Skytop Hill and Other Stories* published by
permission of Chorion Rights Limited

This edition first published by Award Publications Limited 2005

Published by Award Publications Limited,
The Old Riding School, The Welbeck Estate,
Worksop, Nottinghamshire, S80 3LR

10 9 8 7 6 5 4 3 2
20 19 18 17 16 15 14 13 12 11 10 09 08

Printed in the United Kingdom

CONTENTS

The Secret of
Skytop Hill

"Where shall we go today?" said John. "It's jolly cold. We'd better go for a brisk walk."

"Well, let's show Harry the old ruin," said Molly. "The one at the bottom of Skytop Hill."

Their cousin Harry looked at Molly. "What a lovely name for a hill! And what's this old ruin? Let's go!"

"Come on, then," said John, pulling on his coat. "Look, you can see Skytop Hill from here – it's that steep hill sticking up into the sky. It's so wild and steep that nobody ever goes there. The old ruin is near the bottom of it. It was once an inn."

They set off, walking quickly in the frosty air. It took them nearly an hour to reach the old inn, which was indeed nothing but a ruin now.

"People say that smugglers used to run this inn," said Molly, climbing over a tumbledown bit of wall. "It's terribly old – don't you think it *feels* old?"

It did. All the children thought it had a

strange feeling. They wandered about in the ruined building, which had most of its roof off now except for one piece over what had been the big old kitchen.

"Once we played keeping house here," said Molly. "We even made a fire in that old fireplace, and we kept bread and butter in the larder. It was fun!"

"Let's light a fire today and keep ourselves warm," said Harry. "I'll go and get some dead twigs and bits of wood."

But the fire wouldn't burn. John dragged out the twigs and put his head into the grate, looking up the chimney to see if anything had fallen down to block it.

"Sometimes birds build their nests at the top and the bits fall down and stop up the chimney," he said.

"But it's such an enormous old chimney!" said Harry. "Surely no bird's-nest could stop it up?"

"Well – there is something blocking it," said John. "A few bricks have fallen in or some-thing. Wait – I'll poke a stick up and see if I can move them."

He found a long stick outside and poked up the chimney. The bricks were lodged very loosely across the chimney and they fell down into the grate with a clatter and a cloud of dust, making the children jump. When the dust had settled John put his head up again to see if the chimney was clear.

"I say – there's a big space where those bricks fell from," he called to the others. "And I believe I can see something there. Got a torch, Harry?"

"Here you are," said Harry and handed John a small torch. John shone it into the empty space.

"It's a box!" he said, excitedly. "Hidden up the chimney! Whatever's in it?"

"Treasure!" said Harry and Molly together. "Quick, get it down and we'll see."

John managed to get down the box. It was of some kind of metal but it felt fairly light. The children put it on the windowsill, and looked at it. It was locked.

"We must break it open," said John. "Gosh – what a find! I bet there's some kind of secret inside!"

"What shall we break the lock with?" said Harry, red with excitement. "I say, isn't it old and rusty! Whatever was it hidden up the chimney for?"

"There's an old broken poker somewhere," said Molly, looking round. "Yes, there it is. John, smash the lock with that."

Crash! The poker came down on the box. The rusty lock gave way, and the lid hung loose. John opened it.

Inside was a roll of thick, yellowed paper. John picked it out of the box and smoothed it flat. There was nothing else in the box at all.

"It's just an old paper," he said in

disappointment. The others bent over it.

"It's a rough kind of map!" said Harry. "Look – there are the points of the compass shown in that corner – north, south, east, and west. And here's what looks like a road – it seems to fork here and there – but one piece is marked very thick in black ink. That road must lead somewhere."

"Yes – but what road is it?" asked Molly. "It's got no name!"

"Here's something written in this corner," said John. "It's very faded. Wait a bit: Y-E-W-T-R-E-E – that's what it looks like. The road seems to start from there."

"Yew tree!" said Molly. "Well, this was called Yew Tree Inn, wasn't it? But there's no road at all from here except back to Lanning village, where we've just come from. Why should anyone make a map of that and hide it?"

"It's not that road, silly," said John. "We know it doesn't wind like this, and fork here and there – and anyway, on this map the road shown runs in the opposite direction."

"It's strange," said Harry, looking through the window to the north where the road or path on the map was supposed to run. "There's not even a footpath there."

"Listen – there used to be an enormous old

tree, a yew, growing at the corner of the inn!" Molly said suddenly. "It's gone now but the stump is still there. It grew out of the corner of the stable. I remember Daddy telling me about it."

"Let's go and look," said John. So out of the old kitchen they went, and into the tumbledown stable. Broken mangers were still on the wall. The floor was cobbled. A great heap of straw lay in one corner of a loosebox, flattened and brown.

"Here's the stump of the yew," said John, and he pointed to a rotting stump at one end. "Look, they had to make the wall bend in just here, so as not to spoil the tree."

The stump was by the old heap of straw. John kicked some of the straw away – and then saw something odd.

"I say! Look! The floor isn't cobbled here! There's a wooden trapdoor. Do you suppose the road marked on that old map goes underground – could it be a smugglers' way to somewhere?"

"Heave up the trapdoor!" cried Harry. "We'll soon see!"

The trapdoor had an iron handle let into it. John tried to pull it to open the trapdoor, but it would not budge.

"I've got a rope," said Harry, who always carried extraordinary things about with him, just in case they were needed. He undid a rope from round his waist. He slipped it double through the iron ring and threw the two ends over the low wall between the loose boxes. Then the children could pull on it together.

"Now – heave ho!" yelled Harry, and they pulled hard. The trapdoor came up so suddenly that all three of them sat down hard and lost their breath.

John was up first. He peered down into the space uncovered by the trapdoor.

"Steps down!" he cried. "Stone steps. I bet this is the entrance to the secret way marked on that map. It runs north on the map, doesn't it? Well, that means we go right into Skytop Hill!"

It certainly looked as if it did. The steep, rocky slope of Skytop Hill rose up directly in front of them and any underground path must lead into it. How strange!

"Shall we go down?" asked Molly, feeling scared as she peered down into the darkness. "John, do you think it leads to a smugglers' hiding-place – caves or something – you know, where smugglers kept their goods?"

"Perhaps," said John. "Of course we're going down. But if you're afraid, Molly, you needn't come."

"I'm as brave as you!" Molly said, crossly. "Of course I'm coming."

One by one they went down the stone steps. It was a good thing Harry had a torch. There were twelve steps and then a tunnel, dark, narrow, and low in places.

"This is the way marked on the map all right!" said John in excitement. "Shine your torch here, Harry – I want to have a look at the map and make sure I know the right direction. We don't want to go wandering off into any of the wrong forks."

"I hope we don't get lost," said Molly, suddenly feeling afraid. "Harry, have you got some white chalk? You've usually got your pockets full of everything. We could make white crosses on the wall of the tunnel as we go, then if we miss our way we shall be able to find it again by following our chalk marks back to the stable."

"Brilliant idea!" said Harry, and fished a piece of chalk from his pocket. Then on they went again along the tunnel, Harry marking bold white crosses every now and again.

The passage opened out widely after a bit, and here and there other ways ran from it into the hill.

"It's absolutely honeycombed with tunnels!" said John. "Natural ones, too – not hacked out by men. This one looks as if it'll lead right to the very heart of the hill. I say – isn't this exciting?"

The three children groped their way along the passage by the light of Harry's torch. Sometimes the air smelled horrid. Harry kept on marking the wall with his white crosses as he went and the children were glad to think they would be able to find their way safely back again if they were lost.

The passage kept more or less level. John stopped and looked at the map whenever they came to a fork so that he would know which one to take, the one going to the right or to the left.

"We must be getting very deep underground," he said. "The hill must be rising right over us now. We shall soon come under its top."

"I bet that's where we shall find something," said Harry, marking another chalk cross. "I bet that's where the old smugglers hid their goods!"

"We may find some!" Molly said excitedly. "Oh, do come on!"

Suddenly they came into a place that seemed at first to be a great cave – but daylight shone down into it! The children looked round and then up in amazement.

"Why – we're in a sort of deep, deep pit – and that's daylight shining in from the top. There's a hole in the top of Skytop Hill, and it drops right down to where we stand!"

They were quite right. There was a peculiar opening in the top of Skytop Hill, a shaft that went right down to the heart of it, ending

where the children stood. And in the caves round about were many interesting things.

"Boxes!" said Molly. "Crates! Awfully old they look. I'm sure the smugglers hid their things here."

"Look here!" said John, suddenly, and he pointed to the ground. "A cigarette end – and an empty cigarette packet! Now who in the world can have left these here?"

It did seem odd to see the cigarette end and packet lying there among all the old boxes and crates.

"Who comes here – and why?" said Harry, suddenly dropping his voice to a whisper.

But before the others could answer, they heard something that made all of them jump violently. They heard a man's whistle – some-one whistling a tune!

"There's someone coming," said John, in a low tone. "Look – from out of that cave over there. Hide, quick! We'll watch what he does."

The children crouched behind a big, empty crate in the darkness of an overhanging rock. They waited, their hearts beating loudly.

A man came into sight. A broad young fellow, kicking a stone in front of him as if he were bored. He sat down on a box.

The children didn't make a sound. Somehow

they felt that the man wouldn't be at all pleased to know that they were there. They were afraid. "He can't be up to any good," thought John. "We'd better try and find out what he's doing here."

The children crouched silently behind the big crate, keeping their eyes on the man. After a while he left his place and climbed a little way up the side of the pit, where a great rock made a kind of shelf.

Here he tinkered about with something, for the children could hear metallic sounds. There was evidently some kind of machinery up there.

"Molly! Harry! I think that man's a spy or something!" John said in a whisper. "If I get a chance I'm going up on to that ledge to see what he's got there. I can't imagine what it is. If I get caught you must both go back down the secret passage and tell someone about this, and get help."

"Oh, John, don't," said Molly, scared. "Don't climb up to that ledge."

"Shh!" said John as the man climbed down again. He disappeared into a cave. "Now's my chance," said John and darted out from his hiding-place. He climbed quickly to the ledge and stared in surprise. A strange kind of

19

lantern or lamp was there, its face tilted upwards to the sky far above.

"What's it for?" wondered John – and then he heard a warning whistle from Harry. The man was coming again. John tried to scramble down.

But he was too late! The man saw him, made a dart at him and caught him. He shook him so fiercely that poor John thought his teeth would fall out.

"What are you doing here? You'll be sorry for yourself soon!" said the man, and flung John into a small cave. He moved a great crate in front of it. "You'll see what happens to nasty

little boys who snoop around! Have you done anything to that lamp up there?"

The man climbed up to see. Harry ran to free John but there was no time. "Go for help, idiot!" said John. "Quick, before he sees you."

Harry and Molly fled into the secret passage without being seen. How glad they were to know that they had the white chalk marks to follow.

John was left behind. The day went slowly by. He was hungry and thirsty but the man gave him nothing to eat or drink.

And then at night, when it was quite dark, a strange and powerful glow gradually filled the shaft, coming into the cave where John was a prisoner. And, at the same time, there came the drone of an aeroplane engine overhead!

"That glow is from the lamp on the ledge halfway down the pit," said John to himself, filled with excitement. "It can only be seen by anyone flying directly overhead. It's a signal of some sort. What a clever idea – yes, that man is signalling with the lamp – the light keeps going on and off."

The aeroplane droned overhead for a little while, and then made off. The red glow died away.

21

Darkness came again, and poor John trembled in his gloomy prison. If only the others would come.

What had happened to the other two? They had hurried away down the dark secret passage by the light of Harry's torch. Harry held the torch and Molly followed close at his heels.

And then they suddenly lost their way. They took the wrong turn, and when they tried to make their way back, they found they were lost. "I thought we were following your chalk-marks on the wall?" said Molly, almost in

tears. "How did we miss the way?"

Both children were frightened. They sat down to have a rest and to work out which way to go. At last they set out again and after a long time, to their great delight, they came across Harry's chalk crosses on the wall.

"Now for goodness sake don't let's lose them again!" said Molly. "It's getting so late – and I'm starving hungry! It will be dark before we get home."

It was almost dark when the two children staggered in at the back door, and Molly called loudly for her mother. Very soon she had told her the extraordinary happenings of the day.

"I'll ring up the police," said Mrs Johnson, who was astonished and worried. "This is serious. We must certainly rescue poor John!"

Soon the police came in a big car, and off they all went to the old ruined inn. "We had better get to the pit by way of the underground passage," said the inspector. "Something funny is going on inside Skytop Hill!"

They all crept as silently as possible down the secret passage. When they came to the part that opened into the pit they stopped in wonder – for a strange red glow lay all round. It was the glow cast by the powerful lamp hidden inside the hill. Its light shone up, and

could be seen by the aeroplane which was even then droning overhead – but nothing could be seen of the glowing lamp by any watcher out in the countryside!

"A very clever idea!" said the inspector, under his breath. "A fine way of signalling. We've often wondered how it was done. Well, you children have done a splendid job of work for us today!"

Then the inspector and his men took charge of affairs, and things began to happen. The men by the lamp were captured. Other men, hidden in comfortable caves, were routed out and taken prisoner. A radio transmitter and receiver was found that could send and take messages, and these had been flashed to the aeroplane that came twice a week to fly over Skytop Hill. It was a very clever idea.

"Nice little nest of spies!" the inspector said grimly. "Well, well – that aeroplane will have a bad time over here next time it comes. Come along, children – you've had enough excitement for one day!"

"What an exciting adventure," said John, happily, as they went to bed that night. "We never guessed that anything like that would happen when we went to look at the ruin at the foot of Skytop Hill!"

It Happened
One Afternoon

Mike went whistling into his father's study to borrow a map. He and his friend Joe were going on a weekend bicycle tour, and Mike wanted to work out the best way to go.

Mike felt happy. It was a wonderful day, and looked like being a wonderful weekend. He and Joe were to go off that evening, after Joe had finished at the office where he had just started work.

It was half-term. His bicycle was cleaned, ready for the weekend. His mother had already packed him up a bag of food. His father had given him twenty pounds to spend on himself and Joe over the weekend. Everything was fine.

He found the map and slipped it into his pocket. Then he caught sight of a new golf club that his father had bought himself. It stood by the table, neat and shining.

"Ha! Dad's got a new club!" said Mike, and he picked it up. "I bet I could hit a golf ball as far as he can. Wheee!"

He swung it up behind him and brought it down. *Crash!*

Mike turned in fright. He had smashed a lamp and a very valuable vase. There they lay on the floor in hundreds of pieces.

Mike did the first thing he thought of. He shot out of the room, down the passage to the

garden door and out to the shed. He hid there, trembling.

"Dad would be furious if he thought I'd done that," he thought. "So would Mum. They wouldn't let me go away for the weekend with Joe. I wouldn't be surprised if Dad stopped my pocket money."

He stayed there for a long while. He could hear excited voices and knew that the breakages had been discovered. He wondered what to do.

He didn't think of owning up and facing up to his punishment. Let them think it was the cat! Tabs was always breaking something.

He stayed in the shed till teatime. He knew his mother would have gone out by then to see his grandmother. Dad didn't seem to be about either – maybe he had gone for a walk. He wouldn't bother about tea. He would just scribble a note to say he was sorry they were out when he set off for his weekend.

"I don't want to face them so soon after the things got broken," he thought. "I'll just let them think I couldn't say goodbye because they weren't here when I left – and by Monday perhaps they'll have forgotten all about the accident, and won't ask any awkward questions."

He scribbled his note, crept out and snooped around to see where everyone was.

"No sign of Mum, and no sign of Dad either," he thought. "That's good. I'll leave the note on Mum's chair and she'll see it when she comes back."

He left the note, jumped on his bicycle and rode off down the path and into the lane to go to Joe's. His rucksack was on his back, with the things in it he would need. It would be fun!

He rode in at the gate at the bottom of Joe's garden. He gave the whistle that he and Joe used – but Joe didn't seem to be there.

"Blow! There's his bike, all ready – where on earth is Joe?"

He heard a movement behind the little summerhouse nearby, and then a scared and anxious face looked round the corner at him. It was Joe's sister, twelve-year-old Jane.

"Jane! What's the matter?" asked Mike at once. "You're crying. What's happened? Is somebody ill?"

"No," said Jane, with a gulp. "Oh, Mike! It's awful!"

"What's awful?" said Mike, going round the summerhouse, feeling very worried. He was fond of Jane. "Have you gone and got yourself

into trouble, Jane? What have you done? Lost your homework again?"

"No, Mike – nothing like that. It's poor Joe," said Jane, and began to cry again.

"What's happened to him?" asked Mike, impatiently. "He ought to be here, ready to start out with me. Don't say something's happened to stop him!"

"He's not coming," said Jane, almost in a whisper. "He's in awful trouble. He's lost his job at Mr Frost's office. Dad's furious with him and he might have to go to the police station!"

"Gosh – but what's he done?" asked Mike. "Do tell me, Jane. This is awful."

"I don't know exactly what he's done, nor where it all happened," said Jane. "They wouldn't let me stay in the room. All I know is that Joe was sent out to deliver some important papers from the office this afternoon – and – and they say he went to deliver them, climbed in at the window, because he saw a gold watch there – and stole it!"

Mike listened, absolutely amazed. Joe! Why, Joe was as honest as the day. "It can't be true," he said at last. "It's a wicked thing to say about Joe."

"Yes, I know," said Jane, wiping away her tears. "But he was found standing in the room and the watch was gone. They think he must have thrown it out of the window as soon as he heard someone coming. That's what they say."

"But they must be mad," said Mike. "Joe couldn't do a thing like that! He simply couldn't. He must have been in the room for some quite good reason. I know Joe!"

"Joe said he heard a peculiar noise and jumped in to see what it was," said Jane.

"They didn't believe him, of course."

"Look here!" said Mike, feeling very fierce all of a sudden. "I'm going to find out where this place is that Joe's supposed to have stolen the watch from. I'm going to go and see these horrible people there. I'm going to tell them that Joe's my friend and couldn't do a mean thing to save his life! Okay, Jane?"

"Oh, Mike!" said Jane, looking at him with the greatest admiration. "Would you really be brave enough to do all that? You would be a good friend to Joe."

"He's my best friend – and I won't let anyone treat him like that or say things like that about him," said Mike. "What's more, when I've seen these people and told them what I think of them, I shall go and see your father and mother, and tell them they ought to know better than to think Joe would ever do such a thing as steal a gold watch, and tell lies about it."

He got up and Jane got up, too, drying her eyes. "Perhaps they'll let you and Joe go off for the weekend after all," she said. "Oh, Mike – I do think you are wonderful."

"Where's Joe?" said Mike. "Come on – let's find him."

Joe was in his room, feeling very miserable.

Mike went up to him and slapped him on the back.

"Cheer up! I'll go and face these people who say things like that about you! Tell me all about it."

"Haven't you heard all about it?" asked Joe, looking astonished.

"Well – only what Jane's told me," said Mike. Joe went on looking astonished, and didn't say a word. "Do tell me what happened," said Mike. "I want to know so that I can march straight off to these people and tell them what I think of them."

Joe looked at Mike doubtfully. "Well – it seems odd that you haven't heard all about it yet," he said. "I'll tell you exactly what happened. I was told to take some important papers to a client this afternoon. So off I went. Well, as I was walking up to the front door I passed a window and I suddenly heard a most terrific crash. I nearly jumped out of my skin. I looked in at the open window and saw a frightful mess on the floor."

"What was it?" asked Mike.

"I don't really know," said Joe. "Anyway, I stood there wondering what had caused all the noise and mess and thought I'd better investigate. So I jumped in at the window – but

I hadn't been there more than a moment before in came the owners, and shouted at me to know what I was doing there, and what had I smashed."

"Go on," said Mike. "What horrible people!"

"I was just explaining that I'd jumped in merely to see what was happening when somebody called out that a gold watch was missing – it had been left on the table and it wasn't there. So they thought I'd taken it – got in at the window, you see, knocked over a heap of things, and then got frightened and chucked the watch away."

"I call this all absolute rubbish!" Mike said fiercely. "If they knew you they'd never say things like that about you, Joe."

"Actually, they did know me," said Joe. "But it didn't make any difference. They rang up Mr Frost and told him what they thought I'd done, and when I got back to the office, he was very angry at my behaviour and sacked me – gave me my money and sent me off straight away. My father's furious."

"I'm going to see these awful people," said Mike. "Who are they? Tell me their name and address, Joe."

Joe didn't say anything. He went very red and looked at the floor.

"Go on, Joe – tell me quickly," said Mike.

"Mike," said Joe in a low voice, "it – it was your house and your family. You see, I thought I knew you well enough to leap in at the window to see if anything was going wrong – I didn't realise they'd think I'd smashed those things, and taken the watch."

Mike sat down suddenly. He stared at Joe. A horrid sick feeling came over him, and thoughts raced through his mind. He knew at once what had happened.

Joe had just been passing his house when he, Mike, had smashed the vase and the lamp with his father's golf club. Joe had leaped in to see what the noise was – and had found nobody there, because Mike had run straight out of the room and hidden. The gold watch? Yes, it had been there all right – but probably Mike had hit that, too, and quite likely it was in some dark corner of the room, smashed to bits.

He sat staring at Joe, feeling wicked and very miserable. Joe had been punished for something he, Mike, had done and had run away from. Joe had lost his job. Joe was in disgrace. Their weekend was ruined. What was to be done?

"You see – you won't go and face those

people now," said Joe miserably. "They're your own parents. They wouldn't believe even you!"

Mike stood up, very pale. "They will believe me," he said. "And you'll get your job back, and your father will be very sorry he was angry with you. You'll see! But we shan't go off for our weekend. And shall I tell you why? It's because you'll never want to see me again after today!"

He went off, leaving Jane and Joe very surprised and puzzled. He knew what he had to do. He had to do the thing he had run away from that afternoon. He had to go and own up and take his punishment.

He went straight home and found his father. "Dad," he said, "ring up Mr Frost and tell him to take Joe back at once. I'm the one to blame."

"Now, what exactly do you mean, Mike?" said his father, astonished.

Mike told him. "I came in here and saw your new golf club. I swung it – and smashed the lamp and the vase. And I was a coward and ran off to hide in the shed. I hoped Mum would think it was the cat who had broken the things. I didn't know Joe was going to be blamed."

His father listened in silence, his face very

grave. "What about the gold watch?" he said. "That's missing, as you know."

"It's probably lying in the grate, or under the bookcase, smashed," said Mike. "I may have hit that too and sent it flying. I'll look, Dad."

He looked – and sure enough the watch was under the bookcase, badly damaged. He laid it in front of his father in silence.

"Punish me twice," said Mike. "Once for

doing all this and once for making the blame fall on someone else. I know I'm a coward and you're ashamed of me. I'm ashamed of myself. I've lost your good opinion, and I shall have lost Mum's trust – and I've certainly lost Joe's friendship. I'm a – a worm."

"Yes. I rather think you are," said his father. "The only good thing in the whole affair is that you owned up when you saw that Joe was being punished. I'm very disappointed in you. It will take you a long while to get back my trust and make me proud of you – and your mother will think the same. Now go and tell your mother I need to speak to her."

Mike was in for a very bad time indeed. His father would hardly talk to him. His mother looked as if she was going to burst into tears each time she looked at him. Mr Frost turned the other way when he met him.

But would you believe it, Joe didn't turn against him! He was just the same as usual, friendly, kind and generous.

"Idiot!" he said, when Mike thanked him for being so decent. "Aren't I your friend? You're in trouble and you want help. All right, that's what a friend is for. Come on, we'll face this together, and when everyone sees us about as usual, they'll soon forget what's happened.

You were a coward – but you were jolly brave, too, to go and own up just for me."

Things will work out all right, of course, but what a good thing for Mike that he had a friend like Joe!

A Circus
Adventure

One day the circus arrived at Little Carlington. As it came by all the village children ran beside it, cheering and shouting in excitement.

"Look at the great big elephant pulling that caravan! See him waving his trunk about!"

"I say, is that a chimpanzee? Why, he's all dressed up! He's wearing a jersey and trousers and a straw hat!"

"Look at the monkeys peeping out of their cages! Oh, there's one sitting on that man's shoulder – it's dressed like a little old woman!"

"Here come the horses – aren't they beautiful, and don't their coats shine?"

A caravan passed by – very smart, painted in yellow with blue wheels and a blue chimney. A boy sat at the front, driving the horse. Beside him was a girl with curly hair and brilliant blue eyes. Between them sat a terrier, a bright-eyed dog with a tail that never stopped wagging!

The boy was Jimmy, the girl was Lotta. Both

belonged to the circus, and Lucky was Jimmy's clever little dog, who went into the circus ring with him each night.

Lotta waved to the cheering children, smiling. Then she suddenly made a face at them. Jimmy saw her and gave her a hard nudge with his elbow. "Stop it, Lotta! I've told you before it's silly to make rude faces. You only make people cross."

Lotta made a rude face at Jimmy. Then she laughed, and patted Lucky. "I expect I'll still be making faces when I'm an old woman," she said.

"You'll be a jolly ugly old woman, then," said Jimmy. "Well, here's our field. We've been on the move for two whole days and nights – it will be good to stay in one place for a few weeks!"

All the caravans went slowly in through the big field-gate. Here the circus folk would put up the great circus tent, with the big ring inside, and the scores of benches for the village people to sit on.

Oona, the acrobat, came up, walking on his hands as usual, his hat on one foot. The village children loved him. Some of the boys tried to walk on their hands, too, but they fell over at once.

Lotta leaped down, and went over to the children. "This is how you do it!" she said, and turned herself lightly upside down. She walked cleverly on her hands, and then turned cartwheels over and over, first hands, then feet, then hands again, just like a turning wheel!

"Oooh!" said all the watching children, staring in amazement.

"You come to our circus and you'll see me doing this all round the ring," cried Lotta. "And I'll be riding horses, too, standing on their backs – and jumping from one to another!"

Sticky Stanley, the clown, came up. He pretended to fall over his feet. He bent down, put his feet straight, and fell over them again. The children roared.

"Come and see Mr Galliano's Circus!" shouted Sticky Stanley, and began to walk on his hands just like Oona, the acrobat, and Lotta.

"Where's Mr Galliano?" cried the children. "Where's the ringmaster? We want to see him."

"There he is!" shouted Jimmy, pointing to a big caravan in front. "Look – he's getting out now. Look out for his whip – it's half a mile long!"

Sure enough, there was Mr Galliano getting out of his magnificent caravan. He was a big man, dressed in a bright red coat, dazzling white breeches, and big black top-boots. He wore a black top hat well on one side, and he smiled through his long, pointed moustache.

He carried a whip with a very long lash. He raised it and cracked it loudly, with a noise like a pistol shot. *Crack!*

All the children jumped. What a whip! Galliano pointed to a spray of leaves at the top of the nearby hedge; then he cracked his whip again and the end of the lash neatly took off the spray of leaves!

"Do it again, do it again!" cried the children, but Mr Galliano shook his head. He raised his big top hat and strode through the field-gate, smiling.

He was the ringmaster, strict, hot-tempered, warm-hearted and generous. When things went well with his circus he wore his hat well on one side. When things went badly, or something displeased him, he wore his hat straight upon his head. Then the circus folk went carefully, not knowing who would get into trouble next.

"Jimmy – help Mr Volla with the bears," called Mr Galliano. "His caravan has got stuck in a rut, and the bears are upset."

"Take the reins, Lotta, and drive the caravan into the field," said Jimmy, giving the reins to Lotta. "You know where to put it – next to your father's. I'll take Lucky with me."

Jimmy jumped down from his caravan and

ran to help Mr Volla. The bears inside the cage behind the caravan were grunting loudly. What had happened? Why had they stopped? What was all the excitement?

Mr Volla was trying to get his caravan to move. "Hup, then, hup!" he shouted to his horses. "Hey, Jimmy – go into the bears' cage and keep them quiet. I can hear Dobby getting in a fine old state!"

Dobby was the youngest of his five bears, a funny, clumsy, loving little bear. Jimmy was very fond of him. He undid the doors of the cage and went in, closing them carefully

behind him. Lucky slipped in, too. All the animals loved Lucky, and not one of them had ever tried to harm her.

"Dobby, don't be silly! What's up?" said Jimmy, going to the little bear, who was padding up and down, scared. The other bears grunted. Dobby went over to Jimmy and hugged his leg. Jimmy sat down in a corner and the little bear clambered all over him, grunting happily.

Grizel, a big bear, lumbered over, half jealous. She tried to push Dobby away, but Jimmy gave her a friendly punch.

"No, keep off. You're too big to clamber over me too. Play with Lucky!" Lucky ran round Grizel, pretending to snap at her. It was a game she knew well. The other three bears sat and watched, forgetting their alarm.

"Jimmy – are you all right? We're getting Jumbo to pull us out," called Mr Volla. "It's the thick mud that's holding us back."

"Yes, we're all right," called back Jimmy. "Dobby's all over me as usual, and Grizel is playing with Lucky. I'll stay in the cage till we're safely in the field."

Jumbo, the great big elephant, was brought up by Mr Tonks, his keeper. "Soon have you out of this, Volla," said Mr Tonks. "I'm sure I don't know what this circus would do without Jumbo!"

"Hrrrrumph!" said Jumbo, quite agreeing. A little girl pressed near, and Jumbo raised his trunk. He blew hard down it and the little girl's hat flew right off her head. She squealed and all the other children laughed.

"Now, now, Jumbo, no tricks," said Mr Tonks. "That little girl won't come and see you in the circus if you do things like that."

"Oh, but I will, I will!" cried the little girl, in delight. "Do it again, Jumbo, do it again!"

But Jumbo was now busy heaving the caravan out of the mud. One big heave and out it came, followed by the bears' cage behind. The bears were jolted, but they didn't mind. Jimmy was there and he wasn't frightened, so why should they be frightened?

Jimmy was a marvel with the animals. They all loved him, and he loved them. Mr Galliano had once said that even tigers would eat out of Jimmy's hand!

Soon the whole circus was safely in the field. Two village boys followed. Mr Tonks shouted at them.

"Now then, you! No kids allowed in the field except circus kids. Get out!"

The boys took no notice and walked

defiantly over to the monkeys' cage. Mr Lilli-put, their owner, was there. He shouted at the boys too.

"Clear off! You heard what was said. No kids allowed here while we're settling in."

"Why? We shan't do any harm," said one of the boys, sulkily. "Think you own the earth, do you?"

Jimmy appeared out of the bears' cage. The two boys eyed him. As he passed them quickly to go to his own caravan, one of the boys put out a foot and tripped him. They laughed. "Must be blind," said one.

"Or some kind of clown," said the other. Jimmy leaped up and swung round, red with rage. He shot out his fist at the boy who had tripped him up and the blow landed on the boy's ear as he swiftly turned his head away.

Then they both turned on Jimmy, and down he went in the mud. But not for long! Old Jumbo, who was nearby, lumbered up, picked up one of the boys with his trunk, neatly threw him aside and then picked up the other boy. He held him squirming in his trunk, yelling out in fright.

The circus folk gathered round, laughing, not attempting to rescue the boy.

"Well what are you going to do with him,

Jumbo?" said Mr Tonks. "Like to throw him into the stream over there?"

" No, no, no!" yelled the boy, wriggling. "Let me go, let me go!"

"Drop him, Jumbo," ordered Mr Tonks, and Jumbo did what he was told, dropping the boy neatly into a thick patch of churned up mud.

The two boys ran off, one almost in tears. "We'll pay you back, you dirty circus crowd!" yelled one boy when he was well out of reach. "You look out – we'll jolly well pay you back!"

"Bah!" said Mr Tonks scornfully, and Jumbo lifted his trunk and sent a loud jeer after the boys. "Hrrrrumph!"

"Now, get busy!" shouted Mr Galliano, suddenly appearing round a caravan. "Where's Brownie? Oh, there you are. Jimmy, go with Brownie and help him arrange the caravans round the field. Lotta, go to your mother's dogs. They want quietening. Bless us all, do I have to tell you what to do, yes, no?" Soon the two village boys were forgotten as the circus folk settled into their new camping-place. Brownie, Jimmy's father, hurried round the camp, giving a hand to everyone, for he was carpenter and handyman to the circus. Jimmy helped.

Lotta stood with her mother's troupe of dogs round her, looking happy. It was fun being on the road – but it was even better fun to be in camp again. The circus would soon be performing once more, and everyone would be happy.

In three days the circus was ready to give its first show. The big top was up, the great tent in which the show was given. Jimmy's father had set out the benches as usual, and done many repair jobs. Lotta's mother and Jimmy's had been busy washing and mending the clothes of the circus folk. However dirty and untidy they looked in the camp, they always looked spick and span in the ring.

"You look such a dirty little grub, Lotta," said Mrs Brown, Jimmy's mother, as the little girl came into her caravan. "Nobody would ever think you were the same little girl when you go into the ring with your silvery wings, fluffy dress and shining hair!"

"Oh, well – that's different," said Lotta. "What about Jimmy? He looks grand enough in the ring, too, when he takes Lucky in to perform. Did you know Lucky is learning a new trick, Mrs Brown?"

"And what's that?" asked Mrs Brown,

54

sewing silver buttons on to a little green cape.

"Well, Jimmy's got ten skittles, each numbered," said Lotta. "And when Jimmy sets them up he calls out a number and Lucky fetches the right skittle!"

"Oh, yes – and she fetches it because Jimmy has rubbed it with a sausage or something!" said Mrs Brown. "Not much of a trick, that! Still, she's a clever little creature – the cleverest dog I ever did see."

"I've just been grooming my horse, Black Beauty," said Lotta. "She's shining like a mirror! Mr Galliano has given me some new plumes for her to wear. Won't she look lovely, Mrs Brown, tossing her head with its big black feathers?"

" She certainly will," said Mrs Brown. "Now, if you're going to chatter for hours, Lotta, just thread a needle and help me sew on these buttons."

"Oh, I'm just going," said Lotta, at once. "Hello – who's snooping round your caravan?"

A boy's face was looking in at the window. "It's one of those awful boys again!" cried Lotta, and shot out of the caravan.

"What are you doing, prying round?" she shouted. "You've been sent away before, you and your ugly friend there!"

"We don't let girls talk to us like that," said the first boy. "You're a dirty little grub. Go and wash your face!"

Now, Lotta didn't in the least mind being called a dirty little grub by Mrs Brown, but she wasn't going to have these boys calling her names! She rushed at them at top speed, and took the first one so much by surprise that he sat down in a puddle. She stooped and picked up a clod of earth and threw it at the second boy. It hit him on the arm.

"Here!" said the boy, angrily. "Stop it!" He swung round at Lotta and caught her arms roughly.

She yelled at the top of her voice and who should come to her rescue but Sammy the chimpanzee! He had been sitting peacefully outside Mr Wally's caravan peeling an orange, and when he heard Lotta's yells he sprang up, dropping his orange in fright.

What! Somebody had got hold of his friend Lotta? Sammy was furious. He raced clumsily over to where the two boys were shaking Lotta vigorously. He flung himself on one of the boys, making an angry chattering noise.

"Oh – who is it – what is it?" yelled the boy. "Here, you, girl – call him off!"

Lotta hesitated. She was very tempted not to

call off Sammy, but she knew he might bite the
boys and maul them. He was so very strong.

Then she grinned. All right – she would call
the chimpanzee off – but she would give him a
little treat!

"Sammy! Stop!" she commanded. "Stand
away! You can chase them if they run."

Sammy didn't want to let these boys go,
but he obeyed Lotta. He stood beside them,
dressed in his jersey and shorts, but his straw
hat had fallen off. He looked very fierce indeed.

"Let's go," said one boy to the other, and
they turned away.

"Wait," said Lotta. "Sammy, go through their pockets!"

Now this was a trick that Mr Wally had taught Sammy to perform in the ring. He kept a packet of cigarettes in his pocket, and a box of matches, and he had taught Sammy to take these from his pocket when he was not looking. Then Sammy lit a cigarette, and the audience always roared with laughter at Mr Wally's comical look of surprise when he suddenly turned round and saw Sammy.

Sammy was delighted to go through somebody else's pockets! He ran his black fingers through the pockets in the two boys' clothes. They stood still, trembling, not knowing how gentle the big creature's nature was, or how friendly he usually was to everyone.

Out came a dirty hanky, a notebook, a stump of pencil, some toffees wrapped in paper, an apple, some bits of string and a penknife; Sammy put them all into his own pockets, grunting in delight. He unwrapped one of the toffees and offered it politely to Lotta.

"Those are our toffees," said one of the boys, angrily.

"Well, they're not now," said Lotta, rubbing

her arm where the boys had held it. "They're Sammy's. Look, here comes Mr Galliano with his whip. I'll tell him about you!"

But the boys were even more scared at the look of Mr Galliano than of Sammy the chimp, and they took to their heels and fled to the hedge, which they scrambled through at top speed.

They felt safer on the other side. They stood and yelled at Lotta. "You look out! There's trouble coming to you, Miss Dirty Grub! You look out for yourself."

Lotta didn't bother to reply. She considered that she had paid the boys back well. They wouldn't come near the circus camp again, she felt certain.

She went to find Jimmy to tell him about the boys. He had been taking the performing dogs for a long walk over the hills. Lotta usually went, too, but she had been very busy getting her horse, Black Beauty, ready for the opening performance that night.

She saw Jimmy coming down the distant hill and ran to meet him. The dogs were let off the leash as soon as Jimmy saw her coming, and ran to meet her, tumbling over one another in their eagerness to reach her.

"Down, Pincher! Down, Toby! Oh, Lucky,

59

don't prance round in that muddy patch! I'll
have to spend ages bathing you, you dirty little
dog – and you were only scrubbed yesterday!"

Lotta told Jimmy about the two boys. He
frowned when he heard how they had held
her by the arms. "I'll look out for them and tell
them a few things," he said. "I wonder if
they're planning any mischief? Do you
remember, Lotta – a boy got into the camp
and let the horses loose one night?"

"Yes. And one of them plunged into the
stream and broke its leg," said Lotta,
remembering how upset she had been. "Well,
if those boys try any tricks like that they'll be
sorry. I think I'll have Black Beauty tethered

60

by my caravan while we're here. You've scared me, Jimmy! I wouldn't like anything to happen to her!"

The circus opened that night, and the villagers from miles around came trooping to see it. Mr Galliano's Circus. Why, it was famous all over the country!

"I hope they've got those monkeys," said one of the visitors. "I saw them before, when the circus came to a town I stayed at. They had a tea party, and they were so funny. One poured a cup of milk down another monkey's neck!"

"It's the horses I want to see," said another. "They dance, you know – waltz in time to the music. Circus horses are always such beautiful creatures."

"I want to see the clowns," said a child. "There's one called Sticky Stanley that my aunt remembers seeing. He put stilts on one day under long, long trousers, and walked into the ring looking like a giant!"

The circus folk were always excited when the first performance came along. Lights blazed out, the band struck up, the ring was freshly strewn with sawdust. People poured in and filled up the benches.

Lotta and Jimmy peeped round the curtains which soon would be swung back to allow the performers to go into the ring.

"It's a full house!" said Jimmy. "Lucky, look out there, little dog. You've got to do your best tonight, for all those people."

"Wuff, wuff," agreed Lucky.

"I shall put on your little soft rubber socks," said Jimmy, "and you can walk your own little tightrope."

"I love to see her do that," said Lotta, patting the excited little dog. "She does so love it too – she's a proper circus dog, Jimmy, isn't she?"

Lucky certainly brought the house down whenever she walked on the little low tightrope specially put up for her by Jimmy. She had a wonderful sense of balance and had never once fallen off. Jimmy was sure she boasted about it to all the other dogs!

Trumpets sounded, and the circus folk sprang into their places behind the curtain, ready for the grand parade round the ring. Tan-tan-tara! TAN-TAN-TARA!

In went the horses first of all, stepping proudly, tossing their plumed heads. In went Sticky Stanley and all the other clowns, tripping each other up, performing ridiculous

somersaults, hitting each other with balloons. In went the performing dogs with Lal, Lotta's mother, and in went Mr Volla with his bears, little Dobby shambling along hand in hand with him.

Lotta went too, on her lovely Black Beauty. Jimmy followed, with Lucky prancing round him, a bright pleated ruff round her little furry neck. What a brave, happy show they were, and how the people cheered and clapped.

That first performance was a grand success. Everyone clapped till their hands were sore. Jimmy and Lotta had to come on again and again and bow.

"Everyone loves my little Lotta!" said Lal, proudly. "Everyone is clapping her."

But she wasn't quite right. Two people were not cheering for Lotta, or clapping her. Two people were angry at her success that evening.

They were not in the big tent. They were outside, peering through a hole that they had made with a knife. Nobody saw or heard them. They were the two boys who had worried Lotta that morning.

"Bah!" said one, when they spied Lotta through the hole in the tent. "That dirty little grub again!"

The boys watched right to the end of the

show. The night was very dark, and they were well hidden in the shadows. "Better look out now, Ed, in case anyone sees us when they come out of the show," said one.

"We're all right, Jeff," said Ed. "We can mix with the crowd."

They did mix with the crowd, sauntering along as if they, like everyone else, had paid for their seats and had sat in the big tent.

They followed Mr Lilliput as he took his monkeys to their cage, and shut them in. He put Jemima with them, too, because he knew he would be busy for a while.

The two boys stood back in the little crowd and watched. They saw Mr Wally come along with Sammy the chimpanzee, and go to his caravan too.

He put Sammy in. Sammy lived with Mr Wally. He had a bunk in his fine caravan, and Mr Wally treated him just as if he were a child. Sammy dressed himself each day, brushed his fur and washed his face. It was really marvellous to watch him.

Sammy didn't want to be left by himself in the caravan. He was excited by the circus performance. He loved the crowds, the lights, the cheering and the clapping. He sat on the bunk, picking at the sheet there.

He should have begun to undress himself, but he didn't.

Ed and Jeff watched Mr Wally shutting the chimpanzee into the caravan. They noticed that he didn't lock it, but merely slid an outside bolt to keep the chimpanzee inside.

Ed looked at Jeff, raising his eyebrows. Jeff nodded. A little shiver of excitement ran down his back. He and Ed were always on the lookout for mischief – and now, here was some, right under their noses!

They could slip the bolt and open the chimp's door! Nobody would know. It was dark just there, and the people had now gone to see the beautiful horses being led out of the big tent.

Ed climbed up to look into the window of the caravan, but it was dark inside and he could see nothing. Sammy could see him, though, dark as it was! The chimpanzee had eyes as sharp as a cat's at night. He sat quite still, his eyes on the window.

He heard a little noise at the door, and he looked there. Was it Mr Wally coming back? No, it didn't sound like him. He heard the bolt outside being slid back slowly and carefully.

Then the door moved a little, and was left

slightly ajar. Sammy sat and listened, puzzled. Who was out there? He didn't like it. He made a small grunting noise and bared his teeth. If any enemy was going to come in, Sammy was ready for him!

But no enemy came. Instead, stealthy footsteps moved silently away, as the two boys left the caravan, nudging each other as they went, delighted with the mischief they had done.

They came to the caravan where the monkeys were. From inside came an excited chattering and bickering. The monkeys, like the chimpanzee, were excited. They were talking over the thrills of the evening. Little Jemima, Mr Lilliput's greatest pet, watched eagerly for him to come back.

Then she would throw herself at him, sit on his shoulder, cuddle into his neck and nibble his ear lovingly. But Mr Lilliput didn't come. He was always busy on the first night of the circus opening.

The two boys heard the excited monkeys. They nudged one another. Was this caravan unlocked, too? Could they open this door and hope that the monkeys would all escape?

"We mustn't be caught," whispered Ed to Jeff. "We'd get into terrible trouble if we were."

"We could always say that we saw that girl and that boy – what's his name? – Jimmy – we could say we saw them opening the vans," whispered back Jeff. "Feel along this door, Ed – is there an outside bolt?"

There wasn't, but, on the other hand, the door was not even locked. It was just closed, for not one of the monkeys could open it from inside. Mr Lilliput knew that none of the circus folk would go to his van, and he rarely locked it when he knew he was coming back in a short while.

Jeff found the handle. He turned it quietly. Although it seemed to make no noise at all, the monkeys inside heard it, and stiffened. Who was coming in?

Nobody. The door was simply opened a little way and left ajar. The monkeys, silent now, stared at the door. Through the crack they could see the lights that flared over the entrance of the big tent some distance away.

Not far off there came a bellowing snort from Jumbo. He was tethered to a great tree. His sharp little eyes had seen the two prowling boys, and he knew them at once. How did he know them? He couldn't see them clearly, he couldn't smell them, nor could he hear them, and yet Jumbo knew these two boys, and knew too that they had been up to mischief. Clever old Jumbo!

He tugged at his strong rope. It would not break. He gave a mighty "Hrrrrumph!" and made a lot of people jump. But nobody took much notice.

Sammy got out of his caravan first. He went cautiously to the door and pushed it open a little more. He wondered where Mr Wally was. He wanted him. He wanted to be fussed and praised and given the titbits he always had after a show.

He muttered to himself. He would go and find his master. He must be somewhere out there. Sammy could easily sniff him out.

Sammy slipped out into the darkness. He crossed over to the monkeys' caravan and

stopped. What were the monkeys doing? Sammy knew them all and liked them, though they sometimes teased him unmercifully – especially little Jemima, who had taken his straw hat from him dozens of times!

Sammy stuck his nose in the door, opening it wider. He made a few friendly noises. The monkeys knew him at once and Jemima bounded over. She landed on his shoulder and felt for his hat, but he was not wearing it. So she gave his fur a sharp tug and then threw herself to the ground, scampering away in her little coat and skirt at top speed.

All the other monkeys followed, except one who was too tired. They followed Jemima – and she followed big Sammy.

Sammy kept away from the crowds. He was looking for Mr Wally among the caravans, but he couldn't find him anywhere. He came at last to Jimmy's caravan, clambered up on a wheel and peered through the window.

Was his beloved master there, talking with that nice boy, Jimmy? No, he wasn't. Jimmy's mother was there, though, cooking something on her little oil-stove. She looked up suddenly at a noise from the window, just as Sammy slid away from it.

"Good gracious – for a moment I thought

that was Sammy!" she said to herself. "But he'll be safely in Wally's caravan. I'm imagining things."

Sammy lumbered over to the hedge. On the other side he could see people going down the lane. Was Mr Wally with them? He decided to go and see.

He squeezed through a gap and found himself in the dark lane. The people were all going home together, chattering and laughing. Some carried torches, and shone the beams on the ground to make sure they did not walk in muddy patches.

Sammy walked with them. It was so dark that nobody knew he was a chimpanzee. He lumbered along between a man and a boy, with two women in front.

A woman behind shone her torch on his legs, but he was wearing trousers, so the woman thought he was a little man. Not a single person guessed that a chimpanzee was mixing with them, walking back to their village!

Sammy began to feel excited. This was fun! He hadn't been in such a crowd before, like this, all on his own. He longed to take someone's hand, just as he so often took Mr Wally's.

He slid his hand through the arm of the
boy next to him. The boy thought it was some
friend of his and took hold of the hand. It was
furry! He gave a yell and pushed the surprised
chimp away.

"Dad! Dad! Who's that? He's got fur on his
hands!" cried the boy. His father laughed.

"Oh, you've got the circus on your brain.
You'll be thinking it was the chimpanzee next!"

Sammy slid away, frightened by the boy's

shout. He longed for Mr Wally. He stopped by a bush and wondered what to do. He was lost now, so the only thing was to follow the crowds. He padded on again.

Behind him, scampering along in the shadows, came Jemima. The other monkeys, frightened, had bounded back to the circus field, and were sitting on the roof of their caravan, waiting for Mr Lilliput to come. They cowered down, feeling that they were naughty – they shouldn't have left their caravan! But they couldn't get back into it because the wind had blown the door shut.

Soon Mr Lilliput came, still dressed in his colourful circus ring suit. He was whistling softly, pleased with the evening's success, pleased with his clever troupe of monkeys. He opened the caravan door and shone his bright torch inside.

Only one monkey was there, the tired one, who had fallen asleep. She opened her eyes now and blinked. Mr Lilliput stared round the van in alarm.

"Linda! Where are the other monkeys?" he cried to the only one left. "What has happened?"

Linda chattered and came over to Mr Lilliput. And then the other monkeys on the

top of the van chattered too. Wally went out
and flashed his torch over them. "What are
you doing there? Who let you out? Come in at
once, all of you!"

Down they all came, leaping and scampering. Mr Lilliput watched them. Then he
called anxiously, "Jemima! Jemima, where are
you?"

But his favourite little monkey was not
there. No amount of calling brought her to
the van. Mr Lilliput shut the door, locked it,
and turned round, sick at heart. What had
happened to little Jemima?

And then he heard a loud shout nearby. It
was Mr Wally. He had gone into his caravan
and found it empty. Where was Sammy?

"Sammy's gone!" he yelled. "SAMMY'S
GONE! Come out and look for him, all of you.
He's gone!"

"So has Jemima!" called Mr Lilliput,
running up. "Get Mr Galliano, Wally. This is
serious. If they've gone with the crowds,
there'll be trouble. Where can they be?"

What a to-do there was at once over the
whole of the camp. Everyone came from their
caravans to hear the news. Mr Galliano strode
over in his white breeches and no coat, and
with his hat straight on his head. Bad luck of

any sort always made him put his hat on dead straight instead of on one side.

"Sammy gone?" he said, astonished. "Wally, we must get him. He'll get scared and might go for someone. We don't want him to be shot by some idiot."

"Oh, no, no!" wailed poor Mr Wally, in the greatest alarm. "Don't say such things, Mr Galliano. Jemima's gone, too."

"Search every corner of the camp," commanded Mr Galliano. "Put on all the brightest lights. Hurry!"

Jimmy was half-undressed when he heard the disturbance. Lotta came to fetch him. "Jimmy! Sammy's gone, and Jemima too. Do come!"

"Sammy's gone?" said Mrs Brown, Jimmy's mother, suddenly remembering the face at the window that night. "Did you say Sammy? I'm sure I saw him peeping in my window tonight. He must have been looking for you, Jimmy."

"Mum – did you really see him?" said Jimmy, an idea coming into his mind at once. "Where's Lucky? – Lucky, come here. You can help. Lotta, nip over to Mr Wally's caravan and bring something of Sammy's here. Quick!"

Lotta was very quick. She came back with Sammy's pyjamas. He slept in pyjamas just as his master did. Jimmy took them.

He bent down to Lucky. "Smell," he said. "These are Sammy's, Lucky – you can smell they are Sammy's. Now come outside with me. We'll find out if you can smell whether Sammy was really here tonight, peeping in through the window – if he was, you can sniff his trail for me, and show me the way he went."

"Oh, Jimmy – that's clever of you," said Lotta. "We must find him. He escaped once before, and he was nearly shot. Sniff about, Lucky, sniff well!"

Lucky knew the pyjamas were Sammy's. He smelled Sammy's footmarks outside the van too. He sniffed round, found the trail and set off.

"He's got it!" said Jimmy, excited. "Wait, Lucky – I must slip your lead on or you may go too fast for us."

Lucky led the two children here and there, and then made for the hedge. He came to the gap where the chimpanzee had squeezed through, and went through it himself, followed by Jimmy and Lotta. Then off he went down the lane, tugging at the lead, following Sammy's fresh, strong scent.

"Clever dog, good dog," panted Jimmy.

"Take us to Sammy. Oh, Lotta, I wonder where he is – and Jemima, too."

Sammy was at that very moment wandering through the town, still followed by Jemima. He had bumped into a very scared old gentleman, who had immediately rung up the police and reported that a "very big monkey followed by a very small one" had just bumped into him round a corner.

"Ah," said the policeman, "is that so, sir? That was a chimpanzee, the big one, sir – just reported lost from the circus."

The old gentleman nearly fainted. A chimpanzee! Worse and worse. He decided to remain in the street telephone box until the animal was caught, even if he had to stay there till morning.

Sammy was frightened and very tired. So was Jemima. Neither of them had the faintest idea of the way back to the circus. Jemima gave a little whimpering cry and Sammy turned round. She leaped on to his shoulder, cuddling into his neck, and the two went on again together.

They came to a wall. Sammy leaped to the top and looked down into the dark garden below. There was a shed or hut at one side. It looked a little like a caravan without wheels to the chimpanzee, as he peered through the darkness. He decided to go to it and creep in there. Perhaps Mr Wally would come and find him.

So he made his way to it and pushed open the door. Inside were some sacks and old boxes.

Sammy thankfully curled up on a sack with Jemima cuddled against him.

Not far behind were Jimmy and Lotta, with Lucky tugging at the lead, going at top speed up and down the streets where Sammy and Jemima had wandered. "What a way they went!" panted Lotta as they both ran after the excited little dog.

Lucky came to the wall on the top of which Sammy had jumped. The trail came to an unexpected end there, of course. Lucky stopped and sniffed all round. No, there was no scent after this.

"Better go into this garden and snoop round," said Jimmy. "Perhaps Sammy jumped up on the wall. That would break his trail, of course."

They cautiously went in at the gate. It creaked and somebody standing under a tree not far off heard it. It was a policeman, and he swung round at once. He thought he saw two shadowy figures by the gate, and went silently over to it. Was it burglars?

Jimmy and Lotta felt themselves pulled along by Lucky at once, as soon as they got into the garden. He had picked up the trail again, of course! He made for the little shed, whining with excitement. He knew he was near to Sammy and Jemima now!

Just as the three got to the shed, and Jimmy was feeling for the door, there came the flash of a strong light full on them, and a stern voice said, "And what do you think you are up to? You just come along with me!"

It was the policeman who had come in at the gate, had heard the noise they made, and now

had caught them in his torch's light. Jimmy almost jumped out of his skin, and Lotta gave a gasp.

"We're looking for a chimpanzee," said Jimmy. "He's quite near here – my dog's on his trail."

"Ho – a chimpanzee!" said the policeman, most disbelievingly. "That's a fine tale, I must say. You're a couple of bad children, no doubt about it – going to break in somewhere, weren't you?"

"No, of course not," said Lotta, indignantly. "We are looking for a chimpanzee. I believe he's in this shed."

"What do you two take me for!" said the policeman, coming right up to them. "Fairytales don't go far with me. You wait till my chief comes along in a minute or two, and try that tale on him. I'm going to take you to the police station, and we'll meet my chief on the way."

Lotta shook off his hand furiously. "Don't! We must find Sammy. Jemima's gone, too. You don't understand how important it is to find them both. I'm sure they are in this shed."

A voice suddenly came from the gate. "What's all this going on? Is that you, Jones?"

"Yes, sir," said the policeman, glad to hear

his chief's voice. "I've got two kids here, sir – about to break into this shed, I should say. Stuffing me up with tales about looking for a chimpanzee they are! Says he's about here somewhere – I don't think!"

"A chimp? That must be the one reported to us a few minutes ago," said the chief. "He's dangerous, Jones. Have you got a weapon of some sort?"

"There's a heavy spade here, sir – and a chopper," said the policeman, startled. He picked up the chopper and gave the spade to his chief. Jimmy was scared. Nobody – nobody must try to kill Sammy – why, he was as gentle as Jemima!

Sammy and Jemima heard the voices. Sammy came to the door of the shed, blinking in the light from the torch.

"There he is – that's a chimp all right!" shouted the chief. "Throw the chopper at him – get him, quick, before he gets us!"

"No, no!" shouted Jimmy and Lotta at exactly the same moment, and they flung themselves on the alarmed Sammy. But to his delight they were his friends, Lotta and Jimmy, and he put his great arms round them at once.

"Stand away from that chimp," ordered the chief. "You'll get hurt. We've got to get him

somehow. And good gracious – is that a baby
chimp behind?"

"No – it's Jemima!" cried Jimmy, in delight.
"Oh, Jemima, you went with Sammy, did you?
Now we've got you both. Please, sir, let us
take them back to the circus. We've been
hunting for them before they came to any
harm. Their owners will be so glad to have
them back."

"I can't let you two children take a dangerous animal like that through the streets," said
the chief of police. "He ought to be tied up.
Here, now, here – what do you think you're
doing?"

"Just taking Sammy home," said Jimmy,
firmly, pushing past the two burly policemen.
"Don't try to stop us – he may bite you. And
don't try any funny games with the chopper or
the spade, because you might hurt us. That's
right, Jemima, you ride on Lotta's shoulder.
Goodnight, sir!"

The policemen couldn't do anything but let
Lotta, Jimmy, Lucky, Sammy and Jemima
pass. The two men drew back in alarm as
Sammy showed his teeth at them, but he was
only smiling!

"Better follow them to the circus to make
sure they're going there," said the chief,
uneasily. So they walked behind the strange
little company, still carrying the spade and
the chopper!

"Wally, Wally! We've got Sammy!" yelled
Jimmy as soon as they reached the camp. "And
Jemima, too! Lucky trailed them for us!"

Sammy leaped on Mr Wally in delight, and
almost strangled him in his joy at being
with him again. Jemima cuddled against Mr

Lilliput, getting right under his coat and vest and against his chest. "Do you feel safe there?" asked Mr Lilliput, fondling her. "How did you get loose? Naughty little Jemima!"

"You did well, Jimmy and Lotta," said Mr Galliano, suddenly looming up in the camp lights. "Always, always you do well, yes! Good children. You shall come to my caravan and share a supper with me, yes, no?"

"Oh, thank you, sir," said Jimmy. "I hope it's sausages!"

"It is sausages," said Mr Galliano. "You like them, yes?"

"This is a nice, happy ending," whispered Lotta, as she walked beside Jimmy to Mr Galliano's grand caravan, from which came a magnificent smell of fried sausages and onions.

It wasn't quite the end of the adventure though – not for the two bad boys, anyhow! They came up the next day to hear what had happened because of their mischief – and who should see them but Jumbo the elephant.

Jumbo looked at them. He remembered their curious behaviour of the night before. Jumbo didn't forget things like that. He didn't in the least like these boys, and he knew they should not be in the circus field.

He lumbered over to them. Before they knew what was happening first Ed was taken up in Jumbo's big trunk and thrown up into a tree – and then Jeff was taken up. He was thrown high, too – but he didn't land in the tree – he landed on top of Mr Galliano's caravan!

And out came Mr Galliano in a rage, his great whip in his hand. "What do you think you are doing, climbing on my caravan?" he roared. "And you, up that tree? You think the camp belongs to you, yes, no?"

And then he began cracking that long whip of his. *Crack!* The lash swept Jeff's boots as he ran at top speed over the field. *Crack!* It caught Ed round the middle of his legs and stung him well and truly.

"Run, yes, run – and come back for more whip if you want to!" bellowed Mr Galliano, bringing everyone out to watch in astonishment.

Crack! The lash whizzed through the air again and caught Jeff on the hand. He yelled.

Crack! It caught Ed on his right ear, and he howled, too. How it stung! And how clever Mr Galliano was, sending the tip of his lash to ears and fingers and ankles as the two bad boys stumbled across the field!

"They won't come back again," said Lotta,
pleased. She was right. They didn't!
How everyone laughed – yes, even Sammy!

The Mystery of Melling Cottage

"Your Uncle Thomas is coming to stay for a day or two," Mrs Hollins said to John. "He's an inspector, you know, in the police force, and a very clever man."

"Goodness!" said John. "Will he tell me stories of how he catches burglars and thieves?"

"I dare say he will, if you ask him," said his mother. "And you mind you behave yourself when he comes! He thinks that young boys ought to be taught how to behave when they're small – then, he says, they wouldn't get into trouble when they're older, and appear in the courts."

John grinned at his mother. He wasn't a bad boy, and he knew his mother was proud of him. "Well, I'll try not to burgle anybody's house or steal anybody's chickens, Mum," he said, "at any rate, not while Uncle Thomas is here!"

Uncle Thomas arrived. He was not in his

uniform because he was on holiday and John felt rather disappointed. He had hoped to see a very grand-looking policeman in an inspector's uniform. But Uncle Thomas was in a tweed suit and, except that he was very big and had a very clever face with a pair of sharp eyes, he looked quite ordinary.

He liked John at once. "Now there's a smart boy for you," he said to John's mother, when the boy was out of the room. "Asks me sensible questions, listens quietly to my answers, and takes it all in. And when I took him out for a walk this morning he noticed quite as much as I did."

"I'm glad," said Mrs Hollins. "He's a good boy too, honest and straight. I'm lucky!"

John heard a lot of his uncle's tales. How this thief was caught, and that one – how a burglar was traced and the stolen goods found – how bad boys are dealt with and punished.

"We learn to use our eyes, our ears, yes, and even our noses, in the police force!" said his uncle. "You would be surprised if you knew how many times a very small thing has led to the capture of criminals."

John made up his mind to use his ears, eyes, and even his nose too, in future, just in case he might happen on something interesting. But although he kept a sharp look-out as he went about, he couldn't really seem to find anything suspicious or strange that needed looking into.

"John dear, take this bundle of old clothes along to Mrs Browning, will you," said his mother, two days later. "She's a poor old thing and lives all alone in Melling Cottage. You know where that is."

"Yes, I know," said John, and put down his book. "I'll go now." He took the bundle of clothes and set off to Melling Cottage. He knew where it was, at the end of a little lane.

On the way he met old Mrs Browning herself. She was a little, bent old woman, with a pale worried face. She had a basket in one hand, and her purse in the other. She was so thin that John felt sure she didn't eat enough.

"Oh, Mrs Browning, good morning," said John. "I was just going to your cottage with these clothes from my mother. Will there be anyone there?"

"No, no, there won't," said Mrs Browning. "It is empty, and I've locked the door. I'll take the clothes with me now, thank you, John, and carry them back home when I've done the shopping."

"Oh no, they're too heavy," said John. "Haven't you got a shed or anything I can just pop the bundle into, till you come back? I could run along to your cottage, put the clothes in the shed, and you'd find them there when you got back."

Mrs Browning hesitated. "Well, yes, there is an old shed," she said. "It's halfway down the garden. You could slip down there, open the door and put in the bundle. Thank you very much."

John said goodbye and went off with the bundle. He came to the deserted lane where Melling Cottage stood. He went down it and saw the little cottage, a tiny wreath of smoke coming from its chimney.

He pushed open the rickety gate and went along the side of the cottage into the garden. Yes, there was the shed, halfway down. He went to it, opened the wooden door and looked inside. It seemed to be full of rubbish, a broken chair or two, a few pots, a spade, and some firewood. John put the bundle of old clothes down on a broken chair and then made his way up the garden again, towards the cottage.

Growing beside the wall was a very tall foxglove. A bumble-bee crawled into one of the flowers, and John stood still to watch it. And then, as he was standing there, he heard a sudden noise from inside the cottage.

It was the sound of people talking! It started
up quite suddenly and made him jump. Who
was in the cottage? Mrs Browning had distinctly said that it was empty and locked up.
Then who was there?

The voices went on. Then suddenly they
stopped and a band began to play, loudly at
first, and then softly.

"What an idiot I am!" said John to himself. "It's not people. It's only the radio."

He was about to go on, when a sudden thought struck him. Surely the radio had started up quite suddenly – it hadn't been on when he first stopped to look at the bumblebee in the foxglove. And then the programme had been changed to another one – well, then there must be someone in the house playing about with it!

It was very puzzling. John wondered what to do. He decided to go and knock at the door and see if anyone came. So he went round to the little front door and knocked loudly. He waited, but nobody came. There was not a sound from the cottage except the radio, which was still playing music.

John left the cottage, still feeling very puzzled. He met little Mrs Browning hurrying home from her shopping. She stopped and spoke to him.

"Did you find the shed all right? Thank you, John, you're a kind boy."

"Oh, Mrs Browning, I hope there isn't anyone in your cottage," said John, anxiously, "because when I was coming back from the shed, I suddenly heard the radio being switched on."

Mrs Browning looked startled. Then she smiled. "Oh, I must have left it on when I went out for my bit of shopping. I'm that careless! No wonder it gave you a start, John. I'm always doing that."

"Oh," said John, thinking that he must have been mistaken. "Well, that explains it, then."

He walked back home. But on the way he remembered that he had distinctly heard two programmes, one after the other, as if the radio had first been on one, and then had been changed to another.

He thought about it. "Perhaps, though, it was just one programme," he said to himself. "I might have heard the end of one part, and then the beginning of the next, which was music. It could easily have been all one programme. And anyway, Mrs Browning seemed quite certain she had left it on."

All the same there was a little nagging doubt going on at the back of his mind. It did seem as if the radio had suddenly been put on – else why hadn't he heard it when he first went down the garden? He decided to look at the *Radio Times*, and see what programmes were on at that particular time.

"It was about ten-past eleven when I was there," thought John, looking at his watch.

He looked up the programmes. On one there was a talk, lasting from eleven o'clock to a quarter to twelve. On another there was a half-hour of dance-band music.

"Well, then, I *did* hear a bit of two programmes," said John to himself. "It's jolly strange. I wonder if I ought to find out a little more! I wouldn't like Mrs Browning to find a burglar waiting for her in her cottage!"

So that afternoon John went along to Melling Cottage again. The smoke was still coming from the chimney. The radio was silent now. There seemed to be no one about at all.

Feeling a little bit uncomfortable, John knocked at the door. He heard a sudden scraping noise from inside, and then silence. Somebody was there, no doubt about it. He knocked again. He heard another little noise, this time from upstairs. Then he heard footsteps coming to the door. He held his breath, wondering who was going to open it.

And, after all, it was little Mrs Browning, looking quite scared! "Oh, John, it's you!" she said, sounding relieved. "Not many people come along here, and I couldn't think who it was. You must excuse my being so long in answering, but I was in the middle of my cooking."

"That's all right," said John. "I – er – I just came to see if you'd found the clothes all right in the shed."

"Oh yes, thank you," said Mrs Browning. "Won't you come in?"

"Well, I don't think I will," said John, feeling rather foolish. "Goodbye, Mrs Browning."

He went away, still feeling foolish. All the same, he was feeling puzzled too. Why had he heard a noise downstairs when he had first knocked, and a noise upstairs when he had knocked a second time?

"I'm making a to-do about nothing!" he

97

thought at last. "Absolutely nothing. I'll forget about it."

But that night, in bed, he began to worry about it again. He felt sure something was not quite right at Melling Cottage. Mrs Browning did look very white and worried and frightened. And recently she had gone very thin, too. Was there anything the matter?

All at once John threw off the bedclothes, dressed himself quickly, put on his shoes and slipped quietly downstairs and out of the back door. He was soon making his way to Melling Cottage. It was about eleven o'clock, and dark, for there was no moon at all.

Down the little lane went John, and came to Melling Cottage. It stood there, a small dark mass by the side of the lane. There was no light in it at all, and no sound from it.

"I'm an idiot," said John to himself. "What did I expect to find? I don't know! There isn't a thing to be seen or heard. I expect old Mrs Browning is in bed and fast asleep. Well, I'll just creep quietly round the cottage once and then go back to bed. I'm really being very silly."

He walked quietly along the side of the cottage, and then round to the back. There was still nothing to be seen or heard in the

black night. John walked softly over the grass at the back of the cottage.

And then he stopped suddenly. He hadn't seen anything, or heard anything – but what was this he smelled?

He stood and sniffed quietly. Somebody quite nearby – sitting at the cottage window perhaps – was smoking a very strong pipe tobacco. John knew it well, because old Taffy the gardener smoked the same, and John had smelled it time and time again when he had sat with Taffy in the shed during the old man's dinner hour.

And now he could smell that same tobacco being smoked again! It was quite certain it could not be Mrs Browning. It was some man, sitting there quietly in the dark, smoking by himself.

It was all very odd and puzzling. Did Mrs Browning know there was a man in her house? She had said she was all alone, a little, bent, old woman living by herself. Perhaps she didn't know there was a stranger there.

John sniffed the tobacco smoke once more and then turned to go home very quietly. He let himself in at his back door and wondered what to do. Should he go to Uncle Thomas and wake him and tell him? Or would Uncle think he was silly?

"I'd better wake him," said John. "Better to be thought silly than to leave an old woman in danger. That man might rob her!"

So he woke up his uncle. The inspector roused himself at once, and sat up, alert and wide-awake. He listened to John's strange little tale. "You did quite right to come and tell me, John," he said. "We'll investigate in the morning. There's something unusual going on in Melling Cottage, no doubt about that. Sharp work, John!"

"But oughtn't we to do something tonight?" asked John. "Suppose that man robbed Mrs Browning or hurt her?"

"I don't somehow think we need worry

about that," said Uncle Thomas. "Get back to bed. We'll tackle it in the morning."

The next day Uncle Thomas went along to see the local police and make a few inquiries. Then he called back for John. "Come along with us," he said. "Then you'll see what the mystery was."

Two policemen were with him. Awed and a little scared, John went along to Melling Cottage with them and his uncle. They knocked loudly at the door. Mrs Browning opened it. She gave a scream when she saw the policemen.

"Oh! What do you want?"

"Madam, I'm sorry – but we have reason to believe that you are hiding your son, who is a deserter from the army," said one of the policemen. "I have a search warrant here. I must search your house."

They went in. John stayed outside with his uncle, looking scared. Presently the two policemen came out again – and this time they had a great lout with them, sullen and cruel-looking. Behind came Mrs Browning, weeping bitterly.

"He had got a hiding-place under the boards of the bedroom floor, sir," said one of the policemen to Uncle Thomas. "He's frightened

101

his poor old mother terribly – made her hide him – and as far as I can make out she's been giving him all her food and half starving herself."

"I told him to go back," wept Mrs Browning. "I begged him to give himself up. But he's never done as I told him, never. I was too scared to say anything. I knew he'd be found sooner or later. I wanted him to go back and give himself up."

"Oh, shut up, Ma," said the sullen youth. He was led off between the two policemen. The inspector stayed to comfort the poor old

woman a little, and John looked at her miserably. How awful to have a son like that!

Mrs Browning saw him. She patted his arm. "You be a good son to your mother," she said. "Don't you turn out like my boy. He's been cruel and unkind to me ever since he was so high. I spoiled him, and this is my reward! Oh, Inspector, sir, I didn't mean to do wrong, hiding him like that but I was downright scared of him and what he might do to me."

"Now, now, don't you worry any more," said the inspector. "You did what you could. You get somebody to come and stay with you for a few days, and you'll soon feel better."

He and John walked home. Uncle Thomas was pleased with his nephew. "How old are you, John – just gone twelve? Well, I'm proud of you. Good, smart work, that. The police have been looking for that young man for some time and have even searched the cottage once before. But he must have heard they were coming and hid in the woods till the coast was clear again."

"Uncle, I did what you said," said John. "I tried to use my eyes, ears and nose!"

"You did very well, Detective John!" said Uncle Thomas. "I shall expect to hear of more cases you have solved in the future!"

The Lonely Old House

Harry, Cathy and Dick had come to stay at their little seaside cottage, not far from Kelty Cliffs. They loved it, because it was so near the cliff-path that led down to the beach, and had such a glorious view of the sea.

This was the third year they had come there, but this time their parents hadn't come. They had gone to Ireland to see the children's aunt, who was ill. So Miss Truman, their mother's old governess, had come to be with them in the cottage.

"I like Miss Truman, but she doesn't really seem to listen to anything we say," complained Cathy. "She's so busy with the cooking and the shopping and the mending that she just says 'Yes, dear, really,' or 'No, dear, really,' all the time."

"Well, never mind," said Harry. "It suits me! We can do just what we like. Miss Truman never seems to mind anything. Anyway, it's gorgeous here."

So it was. The weather was fine and hot, the bathing was good, they had a very old boat of their own, and there were lovely walks all round.

There were no houses near them at all except one. This was a big old house set in tall trees not very far away. Each year it had been empty, and the children now took no notice of it at all. It just stood there, silent and gloomy, with no one going up the drive or down.

And then one day something happened that made the children suddenly take an interest in the old empty house. They went for a walk with Kim, their Airedale. They passed near the empty house, set round with high walls. Then Kim suddenly ran off, barking.

"A rabbit," said Harry. "Poor old Kim. He never will learn that rabbits won't wait for him. Hi, Kim! Come here."

But Kim didn't come, and from his excited barking the children imagined that he really did have hopes of a rabbit. They walked on a little way, and then whistled Kim again.

"Blow him!" said Harry. "Now we'll have to go and drag him backwards out of a rabbit-hole. One of these days he really will get stuck halfway down."

They went to look for Kim, and then
suddenly they came on something they had
never seen before. It was an odd little
tumbledown house made of the white stone of
the district. It stood there among the trees,
covered with ivy and moss, its roof gone, and
its one window without glass.

"What a funny little place," said Harry, going up to it. "Whatever was it built here for?"

"This wood once belonged to that old empty house," said Cathy. "Mummy told me so. I expect it was a summerhouse or something, built for the people who used to live there long ago."

"Kim's inside!" said Dick. "He must have chased a rabbit there. Kim, come here."

But Kim was very busy scratching hard at the floor of the little stone house. The rabbit had run into the house and disappeared. Therefore it must still be there, and Kim meant to scratch up the whole floor rather than lose it! He was a very persistent dog.

He had scraped away the moss and earth from part of the floor. Dick went up to take hold of his collar and then stopped in surprise. Kim had scratched away quite a hole – and at the bottom of it was a flat stone – and in the stone was an iron handle!

"Look – that's a bit funny," said Dick, pointing it out to the others. "See? Kim's scraped away the earth and come to the stone floor – and there's an iron handle in that particular stone flag. I wonder why?"

"Ooh – it's jolly strange," said Cathy at once. "Usually stones with iron handles in them are meant to be lifted up – like trap-doors. Oh, Harry, don't let's go for a walk – let's dig down and explore a bit."

"No. We shan't find anything and we'll just get dirty and tired out," said Harry. "There's probably nothing in it at all. Come on."

"Oh no, Harry, do let's just scrape away all the earth and see if there is anything exciting," begged Dick. "I've read heaps of adventure stories, but I've never had an adventure myself. This might lead to one."

"Don't be silly," said Harry. He was thirteen, and thought the twelve-year-old Dick rather babyish. "Come on, Kim."

"Well, you go for a walk alone!" called Cathy, crossly. "I shall stay with Dick – and maybe we shall have an adventure – and we'll jolly well have it without you!"

Harry snorted and, with Kim at his heels, he went on by himself. Silly kids! Let them stay and make themselves into a mess if they wanted to.

Cathy and Dick stared down at the stone with its iron handle. "Shall we go back and get our spades?" said Cathy, eagerly. "We can't do it with our hands."

"Yes, let's," said Dick. "And we'll bring a torch too."

"What for?" asked Cathy.

"Well – you never know," said Dick. "It's a very good thing to have about you, if you're expecting an adventure."

They soon got their spades and went back again to the little stone house. What a tumbledown place it was! People could not have been into it for years and years.

They began to dig away the earth and moss from the floor of the house. They cleared it all from the stone flag beneath, and then saw that it was indeed meant to be lifted, for it distinctly moved a little when both children tugged at it!

"Gosh! Isn't this exciting?" said Dick, pushing his hair back from his dripping forehead, and smearing his face with dirt. "Wait – I've got a rope. We'll double it and slip it through the iron handle. Then we can both get a good grip on the rope and pull together. We'll never be able to pull the stone up with the handle. It's much too difficult."

Dick unwound a rope from round his waist. He always wore one there, in case of an adventure. Harry often laughed at him, but Dick didn't mind. One day, he knew, the rope would come in useful – and now it had!

He doubled the rope and slipped it under

and through the iron handle. Then he and Cathy pulled with all their might, panting and groaning with their efforts.

Nothing happened. They sat down to get their breath. "Let's run our spades all round the edges of the flagstone. It's stuck fast with soil, I expect," said Dick. "If we loosen that, the stone might come up more easily."

So they dug their spades all round the edges of the stone and cleared out the dirt. Then they took hold of the rope and tried again. And, quite suddenly, the stone moved! It first moved upwards, and then slid sideways and downwards in a peculiar way. It left a hole, dark and mysterious.

"Gracious!" said Cathy, speaking in a whisper, though she didn't quite know why. "Look at that!"

Dick took out his torch. He flashed it down the hole. "Steps!" he said. "Look – stone steps – awfully steep and narrow, though. I say, Cathy – isn't this exciting? Shall we go down?"

"No," said Cathy, half afraid.

"Well – I'm going, anyway," said Dick, and he put his foot down to the first step.

"I won't let you go alone," said Cathy. "If you're going, I'm coming with you. Oh dear – I do wish Harry was here."

"Well, I don't," said Dick. "He wouldn't stay and help so he doesn't deserve to share in this adventure!"

He went down to the next step. Then to the next. There appeared to be a missing or broken one after that and Dick missed his footing and fell. He gave a yell and Cathy jumped in fright.

But Dick hadn't far to fall – only two or three more steps. He landed on some soft earth, afraid that he might break his torch. But luckily he didn't. "It's all right," he shouted up. "There's a step missing, so look out. I'll shine my torch for you."

Cathy got down without falling. Dick flashed his torch round. A dark, narrow passage ran downwards at the end of the steps.

"It looks horrible," said Cathy, with a shiver. "Wherever does it go to?"

"Goodness knows," said Dick. "Come on. Let's find out."

"We shan't meet anything awful, shall we?" asked Cathy, nervously, not quite knowing what she expected to meet.

"Well, we might see a worm or two," Dick said, cheerfully. "Do come on. Can't you *enjoy* an adventure, Cathy? Just like a girl – scared of everything."

"Well, I'm jolly well not scared, then," said Cathy, in a brave tone. "Only – I'd like you to go first, Dick."

Dick had every intention of going first. Down the narrow, sloping passage he went, with Cathy close behind him. It smelled musty and damp. Dick suddenly wondered if the air was good. He had read somewhere that if the air underground was not good, explorers fell down in a kind of stupor and died. Still, he felt quite all right, so maybe the air was all right.

The passage stopped sloping downwards and went along on the level. It no longer wound about but ran practically straight. Dick tried to puzzle out what direction it could be running in – towards the sea, perhaps? But he could not make up his mind.

He kept the torch pointed towards the ground so as to see where to tread. He did not realise that the roof of the passage suddenly sloped down, and he got a terrific bang on the head as he walked into it. He stopped suddenly with a cry and Cathy bumped into him.

"Oh! What's the matter?"

"Look out for the roof – it gets low here," said Dick, and bent his head down to walk under the low part. Soon he came to a halt. His torch showed him more stone steps – this time going upwards.

Up them went Dick, followed by Cathy, who was now wishing to goodness they could see daylight again. They came out into a great, wide, dark place, and could not imagine where they were.

"It's a cellar!" said Cathy, suddenly. "Look, there are old cobwebby bottles over there. Oooh – look at that enormous spider. Dick, don't let it come over here."

"It won't," said Dick. "It's much more scared of you than you are of it! Yes, you're right. We're in a cellar – and if I'm not mistaken, it's the cellar of the old empty house!"

"Do you really think so?" said Cathy, astonished. "How can we get out then?"

"Up the cellar steps to the kitchen, I should think," said Dick, and began to flash his torch here and there to try and find out where any more steps were. He soon found them, in a distant corner. This time they were made of wood, not stone. The two children went up them to a door at the top. It was shut.

Dick turned the handle. It opened into a great kitchen, with a huge range at one end for cooking.

"Yes, it is the old house," said Dick. "I say – what fun! We can come here and play. We'll explore it from top to bottom."

"Will it matter if we do?" said Cathy. "Won't anybody mind?"

"Why should they?" said Dick. "We shan't do any harm or damage. I say, it's good to see a bit of daylight, isn't it, even if it has to come through such dirty windows."

It *was* good to see daylight. A few rays of sunshine straggled through the window nearby and lay on the floor. It was these that showed Dick something which astonished him. He gave an exclamation.

"Look there! Footprints in the dust on the floor! They're not ours, they're too big. I wonder who comes here."

Cathy stared at them fearfully. They looked freshly made. She didn't like them. Suppose there was somebody in the house now. "Let's go back," she whispered. "Somebody might catch us. I don't like it."

Dick was beginning to feel he didn't much like it either. It was scary to be in an old, old empty house – and see fresh footprints in the dust on the floor. The house was so quiet too – as if it was listening for something. Dick clutched Cathy and made her jump.

116

"Come on. We'll go back. We've seen enough. We'll come back with Harry sometime."

They hurried to the cellar door and down the wooden steps. They found their way to the hole where the other stone steps began and went down those into the dark passage. And then somebody jumped out at them from the passage with a yell that almost frightened the life out of them.

The somebody clutched hold of them tightly and yelled again. Then Dick struck out crossly and yelled back. "It's you, Harry, you beast! Scaring us like that. You really are horrible."

Harry laughed. He was very, very glad to find the others. He and Kim had come back to the little stone house and discovered the hole where the stone had been, and the steps leading down. Cross to think that Dick and Cathy had actually discovered something exciting, Harry had gone down after them.

But he had no torch and it was not at all pleasant groping about in the darkness. He longed to hear the cheerful voices of the others – and at last he did hear them! He had waited to jump out at Dick, and had given both Dick and Cathy a terrible fright.

"Sorry," said Harry. "Did I really scare you so? Get down, Kim. Dick, where does this lead

to? You found an adventure after all!"

"Rather!" said Dick. "One up on you! Gosh, I'm glad you're here, Harry, even though you did scare me stiff. Do you know, this passage leads to the cellar of the old empty house! And we've been up into the kitchen – and there are fresh footprints there in the dust of the floor!"

"Whew!" said Harry. "That's strange. Who comes here then? Perhaps it's just some tramp at night."

"But we *know* the place is locked and barred," said Dick, "because we've often tried to get into it ourselves from the outside, just to see what it was like. And we never could. It can't be just a tramp!"

"Let's go back again and I'll have a look," said Harry. So back they went and, once they were in the kitchen, Harry saw the big footprints too.

"Yes – they're freshly-made all right," he said. "Listen, there's somebody opening the front door! Quick, down to the cellar!"

Their hearts beating fast, the children made for the cellar door. They stood there and listened for a moment. They heard the front door open, and then to their great amazement they heard a voice they knew well! It was old Mrs Harriman, who went out doing housework, and who came to them every Saturday to help Miss Truman. Whatever was she doing here?

Kim whined, for he too recognised Mrs Harriman's voice, but Harry's hand tightened on his collar. No, he must not give them away. Mrs Harriman was talking to somebody.

"Well, here we are, Liza, and I must say it's a dreadful place, enough to give you the creeps. Fancy somebody coming along to live in it after all this time. Well, you and me's got our work cut out to clean the place up a bit, and scrub them filthy floors."

Kim whined again, and the children retreated down the cellar.

"Funny," came Mrs Harriman's booming voice as she entered the great kitchen. "I thought I heard a dog whining then. Shows you what your imagination can do!"

Harry shut the cellar door softly and went down the steps after the others. They made their way to the hole and went down the steps into the passage. Soon they had arrived inside the little tumbledown stone house, glad to see the sunshine coming through the trees.

"Well – it wasn't so mysterious after all – seeing those footprints," said Harry. "They must have been made by somebody who came to look at the house. Fancy people coming to live here after all those years! I wonder who they are. Perhaps Mrs Harriman will know."

"Don't tell her about the underground way into the house," said Cathy. "Let's make it our secret. I like secrets like that."

"Course we won't tell her," said Dick. "Let's shut the stone door and pull bracken over it to hide it. It might be fun to use it again before the people come in."

They went home with Kim, who looked very disappointed. He had hoped to find plenty of rabbits down that wonderful dark rabbit-hole

– and there hadn't even been a smell of one!

Miss Truman did not seem to mind their coming home so dirty. She did not even ask where they had been. So long as they were in good health and hadn't hurt themselves she didn't really bother much about their doings.

The next day was Saturday, so the children asked Mrs Harriman, when she came to do some cleaning, if anyone was coming to the old house.

"Yes, there is," said Mrs Harriman, beginning to clean the floor with a large bucket of water and an outsize mop. "My, my, look at this floor! Doesn't anyone wipe their feet in this house?"

"Only Kim," said Cathy, with a giggle. "Who's coming to the old empty house, Mrs Harriman?"

"Well, that I don't rightly know," said Mrs Harriman, beginning to mop vigorously. "Mind your feet, miss. The house agent, he called on me, gave me the key, and said I was to go up and clean, with Liza. All he said was that a gentleman was coming to live there, a real recluse, he called him, though what that is I don't know."

"Nor do I," said Cathy. But the boys knew.

"It's somebody who wants to live away from

everyone and not be bothered by visitors or anything," said Dick. "Well, he won't be bothered much there. When's he coming?"

"Next week, so I hear," said Mrs Harriman. "Mind your feet again, miss. And if anybody treads on where I've just cleaned they won't get any of my chocolate buns for tea, and I tell you that straight."

Everyone immediately went away from the gleaming wet part that Mrs Harriman had mopped. There didn't seem to be much more information they could get out of her, so they retired to the garden where they picked and ate a large amount of purple plums.

"We could watch each day and see who comes," said Dick. "We can see the furniture vans. They will have to pass our cottage."

"So they will," said Cathy. So each day the children watched, and on the next Wednesday they were rewarded by seeing two great vans come lumbering by. They followed the vans up to the old house.

Mrs Harriman was there with a paper in her hand, directing proceedings. "All furniture marked D is to go into the dining-room," she told the foreman. "I'll show you which it is. And all marked K is to . . ."

"It's just the furniture – not the recluse

man," said Cathy, disappointed. "Blow! We shan't see him now."

The children were not interested in the furniture, so they went away. They found their bathing things and went to bathe. They then took out their leaky old boat, got caught in a current, and had to row so very hard back to shore that they were absolutely tired out.

They crawled back to their cottage, groaning and stiff. "Done too much, I suppose?" said Miss Truman. "Well, I'll get you some supper and then off to bed you must go. You'll be asleep in two shakes of a duck's tail, I should think."

The boys were, but Cathy was too tired even to go to sleep! She tossed and turned. She heard the church clock down in the distant village strike ten, eleven and even twelve. She dozed a little and then heard it strike one.

And just as it had struck, she heard another noise. It was a car coming slowly and quietly along the lane by their cottage! Cathy was most surprised. No cars ever came along there, for the lane was a dead end, going only to their cottage and then a little distance on to the old empty house. Was the car going to stop at the cottage?

No, it was not. It went straight on past it, up

the lane. Cathy listened. How very peculiar! Was it going to the old house? But how late at night to arrive!

She lay down again. The car did not come back. She listened for it for some time and then quite suddenly fell asleep.

In the morning she was not quite sure if she had dreamed it. So before she told the boys she went into the sandy lane and had a look round. Yes, there were the marks of the tyres. So she hadn't dreamed it.

"The recluse man has arrived at the old house," Cathy announced to her brothers at breakfast.

"How do you know?" said Harry, disbelievingly.

"Because I heard his car going by last night at about one o'clock," said Cathy.

"That's morning, not night," said Dick.

"Well, it was one o'clock in the morning, in the middle of the night," said Cathy. "And anyway, there are tyre marks in our lane this morning."

The children went for a walk up to the old house after breakfast to see if they could see any sign of the "recluse man", as Cathy would keep calling him. But the great iron gates were not only closed but padlocked, and, as

125

there were high walls all round the grounds, the children knew there was no way of getting in at all. Except, of course, by the underground passage.

"But we can't possibly use that again," said Harry. "Not now the house is occupied. It didn't matter when it was empty. My word, the recluse, whoever he is, means to keep everyone away, doesn't he?"

"What about food and milk and stuff?" wondered Cathy.

"Oh, he's probably got good stores," said Harry. "Come on – let's go and lie on the sand. I'm so stiff with rowing yesterday that I don't even want to bathe today!"

So, with Kim bounding along beside them, the children went down to the beach and forgot all about the peculiar old house. They spent a happy, lazy day together, and went off to bed, yawning, at nine o'clock.

Cathy had tossed and turned for hours the night before, so tonight she fell asleep at once. Dick did too, but Harry lay wide awake, listening to the owls hooting in the woods round the lonely old house. He was glad he was in his cosy cottage, not imprisoned in that great house, surrounded by high walls and tall trees.

He lay so that he could look out of the window. It was very dark outside for the sky was clouded over, and there was no moon at all. He faced in the direction of the old house, which was a good way away, hidden by trees.

Harry lay there, gazing out for a little while – then he became conscious of some far-off light somewhere. Was it a light? He tried to focus his eyes in the direction from which he thought it came, and waited. Yes, it was some kind of light – faint and far off – and coming in flashes. How odd. Where did it come from?

He thought for a minute. It could come from the top windows of the old house. He could see those indistinctly through the tops of the trees in the daytime, if he looked out of his window. But why should a light come and go from there in the middle of the night?

He decided to get up and investigate. He pulled on his shorts and jersey and went out, Kim running beside him, surprised and pleased to have a night walk.

Harry made his way towards the old house. He could not see in the dark, and almost bumped into the trunks of trees as he made his way between them.

And then he saw the light quite distinctly. It came from the topmost window of the old

house, a pin-prick of light, flashing on and off, on and off, as if the owner was trying to signal to somebody. But to whom would anyone want to signal at night, in that lonely place? Nobody would ever see that pin-point of light, except by accident.

Then the light became fainter, and finally the flashes stopped altogether. Harry made a note of exactly where the window would be and made up his mind to look for it the next day. Then back he went to bed and quickly fell asleep.

He told the others the next morning and they felt very excited. "It's a mystery," said Dick. "There really is some sort of mystery. We must solve it!"

They went to have a look at the window. It was the topmost one on the eastern side of the house – and it was barred.

"Well, that's nothing. It's always been barred, as long as we can remember," said Dick. "It was once a nursery, Mrs Harriman said."

"Do you think there is anyone there now?" said Cathy. "I mean – somebody we could see, if we climbed a tree, say?"

"Cathy, that's an awfully good idea!" said Harry at once. "If I climb this tall tree here, its top will be about level with that window. I'll do it."

The tree was a chestnut, and it grew just outside the wall that ran round the grounds of the old house. Harry climbed it easily. He went steadily to the top and then slid out on a broad branch to get as near as he could to the barred window. But he was still so far away that he could not possibly see inside.

And then, just as he was going to get down, somebody came to the window and looked out. Harry expected to see an old man – but instead he saw a young boy with a shock of dark hair, enormous dark eyes and a pale face. Harry was most surprised, and stared across at the window in astonishment. He gave one of his piercing whistles to get the boy's attention.

The boy heard it and looked out. He suddenly saw Harry on the branch of the chestnut tree and was so amazed that he could only stand and stare. Harry yelled to him:

"Who are you?"

The boy put his finger to his lips and looked thoroughly scared. Harry did not shout again. Then the boy made a sign to Harry to wait, and disappeared from the window. He was away for a minute or two then came back.

He put his finger to his lips again, to tell Harry not to make a noise. Then he began to hold up sheets of white notepaper, on each of which he had printed in bold black letters one letter of the alphabet. He held them up one after another for Harry to see.

Harry jotted them down in his notebook as the boy held them up. I-A-M-A-P-R-I-S-O-N-E-R. It was not until he had got them all jotted down that Harry suddenly saw what words they spelled. "I am a prisoner."

"Golly!" thought Harry. "So that's what the light meant last night. He was signalling with his torch, I suppose, hoping someone would see the light, till the battery failed. Gosh, what am I to do about this? How can he be a prisoner?"

Harry waved reassuringly to the boy, and
was just about to begin climbing down the
tree when he saw that the prisoner had
disappeared very suddenly indeed from the
window. Then a furious face appeared and
looked out. It was the face of a bearded man
wearing big glasses, with black frames.

Harry slid out of sight at once. He climbed
down as quickly as he could and told the others
what he had seen. They listened breathlessly.

131

"Then it is an adventure," said Dick. "I had a feeling we were in for one. We'll have to rescue this boy. Perhaps he has been kidnapped."

"Yes. I never thought of that," said Harry. "We'd better look in the paper and see if there's anything about kidnapping. We never usually look at the paper, so we wouldn't know."

They went back to the cottage, and on the way they met Mrs Harriman, going to clean at the old house.

"Mrs Harriman – have you seen the man at the house?" asked Harry. "Is he all alone?"

"Yes, not a soul there besides himself," she answered. "Says he's writing a book and has to be quiet and by himself."

"Are you sure there's nobody else?" asked Dick. "Have you been all over the house?"

"Of course I have," said Mrs Harriman. "Not on the top floor, though, because there's nothing there, so Mr Cordery says."

"Oh – that's what he says, is it?" said Harry. "Well, Mrs Harriman – just suppose I told you there was a prisoner up there?"

Mrs Harriman laughed loudly. "Now don't you go playing any more of your jokes on me, young Harry. I've had enough of them. If you think you're going to make me climb up those steep stairs to the top, just to look for an imaginary prisoner, well, you can think again. You and your imaginings!"

And she went on her way, chuckling. It was no good trying to get any advice from Mrs Harriman, or any help either. They went in at their cottage gate and went to look for the paper.

And there, the headline, big and black, stared them in the face: JACKIE MACARIO, SON OF FAMOUS FILM STAR, KIDNAPPED. The children gazed at the words as if they couldn't believe their eyes.

"Do you think," said Cathy at last, in a whisper, "do you think that's the boy – the one Harry saw?"

"Yes," said Dick. "Miss Truman, did you see this in the paper this morning – about the kidnapping? Well, we know where the boy is."

"Now, don't tell silly stories," Miss Truman said placidly. "If you want to pretend things and play games like that, you can – but really you can't expect me to believe them!"

And the more the children told her about what they knew, the more she pooh-poohed it all. She could not realise that they were no longer small children, and she wasn't going to be bothered to go into their ridiculous tales.

"It's no good," said Harry, at last. "We'd better do something ourselves. We'll rescue him tonight."

"How?" asked Dick at once.

"We'll go through the underground passage, into the cellar, up into the kitchen, and up to the top floor," said Harry. "The door will be locked and bolted – but the key and bolt will be on the outside, and we can easily undo them."

"Oh – I'd be afraid!" said Cathy.

"Well, don't come then," said Dick. "I'll go along with Harry – and we'll take Kim too."

"Oh no, I must come if you go," said Cathy bravely. So they laid their plans, and waited anxiously for the night to come.

At eleven o'clock they set out with their torches. Kim went with them. He had been warned not to bark and he quite understood. The three children came to the little tumbledown summerhouse and removed the flagstone that hid the entrance underground. Down they went, one by one. Cathy was trembling. It was so dark and spooky. She was glad to feel Kim's tongue on her bare legs now and then.

Along the passage, up to the cellar, up the wooden steps to the vast dark kitchen, where a winking red eye showed where the great range was almost out. Then out of the kitchen and into the hall.

The wide stairs lay before them, well carpeted. Where was Mr Cordery? In his room, probably. There was no light to be seen anywhere.

The three went up the stairs with Kim beside them. It seemed as if he, too, was walking on tiptoe! Up one flight of stairs – up

another – and then a third. Now they were at the very top of the house.

Harry quickly swung his torch around the top landing. All the doors were open but one. The prisoner must be in that!

They tiptoed towards it. It was bolted. There was a large key in the lock, and the children felt sure the door was locked too.

Cautiously Harry turned the key. It gave a slight click. Then he slid back the bolt. It creaked a little, and the children held their breath as they waited to see if anyone had heard. No, there was no sound.

Harry turned the handle and pushed the door open. The room was in darkness. Then a scared voice came from somewhere. "Oh, what do you want? Why do you keep me here like this? Don't hurt me, don't hurt me!"

It was a boy's voice. Harry switched on his torch and spoke in a whisper.

"Are you Jackie Macario?"

"Yes, yes. Who are you? Oh, don't scare me so!"

"We are your friends," said Harry. "We've come to rescue you. I'm the boy you saw in the tree – the one you showed those letters to."

"Oh, yes – I got beaten for that," said the boy. "Have you really come to rescue me? Let's

136

go then, before that horrible man discovers you."

Without waiting to put on even a dressing-gown the boy went to the door with the others. He jumped violently when Kim licked him for he had not known there was a dog there.

"It's only Kim," whispered Dick. "Come on. Down the stairs."

They went down the stairs as quietly as possible. But suddenly, in the darkness, Cathy bumped into something and it fell over with a crash. Scared almost out of their skins, the four children ran swiftly across the landing to the next flight of stairs.

And then suddenly a door was flung open, a light flashed on, and there was Mr Cordery, black-bearded and fierce, glaring at them in the greatest astonishment.

"What's this? Who are you? Come here, you, you, you . . ."

He was in such a rage that he could not get his words out. He caught hold of Dick and shook him hard.

The others paused, afraid for Dick. Kim gave a growl and flung himself at Mr Cordery. The man gave a shout and tried to fend the dog off.

"Come on, Dick!" shouted Harry, running

down the next flight of stairs. "Leave Kim to settle him." They had enough time to dart into the kitchen. Then Kim came after them, his head bleeding from a savage blow. Then came Mr Cordery raging with temper, an iron bar in his hand. The children ran to the cellar door and down the wooden steps. Kim followed them.

The door slammed above them. They heard Mr Cordery's loud laugh. "Ha! You want to be prisoners, too, do you? Well, you shall all stay down in the cellar, in the dark and cold, with the spiders and the bats!"

Then the key turned in the lock of the cellar door. Harry began to laugh weakly. "He thinks we're his prisoners. He doesn't know it's our way of escape. Come on, quick, before he smells a rat!"

They dragged the surprised and frightened boy with them. Down the steps, into the underground cellar, along the passage and up into the old summerhouse. Then through the woods and home. Cathy was terribly worried about poor Kim. Was he very badly hurt?

They went into the house and banged on Miss Truman's door. "Miss Truman! Come quickly!"

Miss Truman came, looking most astonished. When she saw the three bedraggled children, and a fourth one, quite strange to her, and poor Kim bleeding from his wound, she was quite astonished.

The children poured out everything to her.

"Oh dear, oh dear, why didn't you tell me before?" she said, as she bathed Kim's head.

"But we did, and you thought we were making it all up," said Cathy, quite crossly. "Miss Truman, oughtn't we to tell the police? Jackie Macario's mother and father ought to know where he is, and the police ought to know about Mr Cordery."

"Of course, of course," said Miss Truman, putting her arm round the shivering Jackie. "You go and get a dressing-gown for him, Harry. Kim will be all right now. I'll go and phone. Dear me, what a night, what a night! I can scarcely believe it!"

Neither could the local policeman when Miss Truman telephoned him. But he did believe her tale at last, and said he would telephone his superior officer in the next town and get instructions.

And before very long a police car came roaring up with a detective and three big policemen in it, all very anxious to see for themselves if the little prisoner the children had rescued really and truly was Jackie Macario.

Nobody had much sleep that night, except little Jackie who was tired out with excitement.

The police left the cottage and roared on to

the old house. Mr Cordery was astounded to hear loud knockings on the front door, and only when he heard that it was the police who were demanding entrance did he open the door.

And then it was Mr Cordery who was taken prisoner!

"I tell you I know nothing about Jackie Macario," he kept saying. "Nothing at all."

But when he was faced with the boy the next day, he could no longer go on with his tale. "All right," he said, sullenly. "I'll tell you everything. I didn't kidnap him – the others did that. I just brought him here and put him in that barred room to wait till the ransom was paid. That's all I did. And then some interfering kids got him away – though how they got into the house, and out of the cellar I locked them into, beats me!"

"Yes. A clever lot of kids," said the detective, smiling round at the three children. "Well, Jackie, your parents will soon be here, and you'll be safe again."

"I'd like to stay with these children if Mum will let me," said Jackie. But alas, she wouldn't. She took her precious son away with her, thankful to have him safely back – but she left behind three things that thrilled the children tremendously.

One was a great rubber ball for playing about with on the beach or in the sea. That was for Harry. Another was a shrimping net almost as big as the one the fishermen used when they went shrimping. That was for Dick. The third was a funny rubber horse that could be ridden in the waves. That was for Cathy.

"Gracious!" said Cathy, in delight. "What great presents – and all for taking part in a really exciting adventure. Miss Truman, you can have a ride on my horse if you like, next time you bathe."

"No, thank you," said Miss Truman, eyeing the big rubber creature in horror. "I know what would happen to me! I'd be pushed off it at once – that would be your idea of a joke!"

The children laughed and raced off to the beach with their presents. "Let's hope for another adventure soon!" said Dick. "They're *fun*!"

Number
Sixty-two

Ever since John had solved the mystery of Melling Cottage he had been on the lookout for another. But mysteries didn't seem to come along very often – and some mysteries turned out not to be mysteries after all!

There was the time when he had seen a man and a woman quarrelling in a garden, and suddenly the man pulled out a knife, but when John yelled out that he was going for the police it turned out that the two were only rehearsing their parts in a play.

John had felt very foolish over that. And another time he had reported a mysterious sack on the other side of a hedge, apparently full of stolen goods. But it was only a sack of potatoes left there by the farmer for his brother to fetch as he passed by on his way to market.

"I'd better be careful next time," John said to himself. "I won't report anything unless I'm absolutely sure about it."

Now one afternoon he went by himself to Oaktree Wood. There was a big tree there he liked to climb. It was an easy one and he could get almost to the top. From the top he could see a very long way indeed.

It was like being in a ship, because the wind swayed the tree, big as it was, and the movement was like a boat going over waves. John liked it. If he shut his eyes he felt as if he were right out at sea.

So this afternoon up the tree he went. He was soon at the top, looking out over the countryside, which lay smiling in the summer sunshine. John had a book with him. He opened it, settled himself comfortably on a branch and began to read. Sometimes he looked out from his high perch, and saw the lorries, buses and cars going along the roads.

He saw a car stop and pull off the road on to the grass verge. A man got out and disappeared. John waited idly for him to come back, but he didn't. Surely he hadn't gone for a picnic all by himself? John went on reading his book, occasionally glancing up to see if the car was still there.

After half an hour the car was still parked there, empty. John began to wonder about it. Then he suddenly heard the crack of a twig in the wood below, as if someone had trodden on one and broken it.

"There's somebody coming through the wood," thought John, and glanced down through the leaves. But the tree was too thick for him to see anything below on the ground.

He heard a match being struck. Somebody was lighting a cigarette. Perhaps he was waiting for someone! John heard a slight cough down below. The man was under the tree. Another twig cracked.

Then there came the sound of someone making his way through the bushes, and a low voice said, "That you, Lou?"

"Yes," said the man under the tree. "Number 62, tomorrow."

"Okay," said the other voice and its owner made his way back through the bushes again. That was all. Not another word was said. The man under the tree went off and in about ten minutes' time John saw him come out of the wood and get into the car.

John strained his eyes to see the number of the car. He could make out the beginning – L39, and the last two letters, which were ST, but that was all. He wrote it down in his notebook.

Car number L39 . . . ST, he wrote. *Red in colour. Sports saloon. Can't see make.*

John often wrote things of this kind down but as a rule they were all wasted. Still, you never knew. Things might come in useful sometime. He began to think about the message the man under the tree had given to the other, who was, apparently, already hidden in the wood.

"Number 62, tomorrow."

What did it mean? What was number 62? And why tomorrow? John frowned, and puzzled over it. Should he report what he had seen and heard? No, better not. It might be nothing again.

"Perhaps number 62 is a house somewhere they mean to burgle," thought John, suddenly. "Number 62. Where is there a number 62? It must be a fairly long street if there are over sixty houses in it. I'll go and do a little exploring."

Before he slid cautiously down the tree, he listened to see if anyone might be about – the man hiding in the wood for instance. But he could hear nothing, so down he went, as quietly as he could. Once on the ground he sped through the trees as if he were a rabbit with a dog after him!

He went to the village. There must be a number 62 somewhere. What was the longest road? Yes, Summers Avenue must be. He went along it, looking for sixty-two.

"Forty-one, forty-three, forty-five – oh, these are the odd numbers. I want the evens." He crossed the road and came to the evens.

"Forty-two, forty-four, forty-six – blow, there are only two more. Forty-eight – fifty. There's no sixty-two."

He went down another street but there were even fewer houses there. That was no good. Then he went to Limmers Street, which was a terrace of small houses. Ah, there was a sixty-two – good! John looked hard at it.

Nobody would want to rob a tiny house like that, surely? The people in it must be very poor for the curtains were dirty and ragged. Two or three equally dirty and ragged children were playing on the doorstep. No, this couldn't be the right sixty-two. That was quite certain.

"Well, there's only the High Street left then," thought John, and went there. However, he felt that number 62 could hardly be the one meant by the man, for it was the police station! It had no number, of course, but as it stood between number 60 and number 64, it was clear that it must be 62, if it had a number at all!

"I can't understand it," said John, puzzled. "There are only two sixty-twos – and one's a slummy little house and the other's the police station. Perhaps the sixty-two doesn't mean the number of a house at all."

Then he wondered if by any chance the number might be part of a telephone number. No – the man wouldn't have said "sixty-two" then, he would have said "six-two" because that was how telephone numbers were given. People said "one-o" not "ten," they said "seven-three" not "seventy-three" and the man would certainly have said "six-two" not "sixty-two".

So telephone numbers were ruled out as well. Then what in the world could sixty-two mean?

Should John go to the police now, and tell them what he had heard? No, he still didn't want to, because it just might mean nothing, and he would be laughed at.

He turned to go home. On the way he saw a man running by in a white tee-shirt and shorts. Then after a while another came past. They were practising running for races. John stared at them idly. Then he stiffened. Each man had a number on, in big black figures! The first man's number was 14. The next

man's was 34. Then a third man came padding along – he was 53.

John looked after the runners. Could the number 62 belong to one of these runners? Was it a man, number 62, that that fellow was talking about? If so, why?

He went on towards his home, thinking hard. His father was at home. Perhaps he would be able to tell him about the runners and their big race.

Yes, his father knew all about it. He had been a keen runner in his time, and he told John that there was to be a ten-mile race the next day, on a certain route, and that so far as he knew almost a hundred competitors were entered for it.

"Then there may be a number sixty-two?" asked John.

"Yes, of course. But why do you ask that?" said his father.

"Oh – I was thinking of something," said John. "Dad, is there a list of the competitors up anywhere? If there is I'd like to have a look and see if I know any of them."

"Yes. If you go along to the athletic club, you are sure to find a list there," said his father. "I didn't know you were so interested in running."

John smiled and went off. He found the athletic club and went in. The secretary was there. "What do you want, young lad?" he asked.

"Could I just look at the list of runners?" said John. "For the ten-mile race tomorrow?"

"Yes, it's over there," said the secretary, and pointed with his pen. "They start at Beamers End, each running two minutes after the last. And they end at Longfields Club Room."

"Er – do they run past Oaktree Wood?" asked John. The secretary nodded. John began to look down the list of names. He came to number sixty-two: 62. Laurie Baxter. Who was Laurie Baxter? He looked at the address: 16 Renfrew Street. That was a poor street, where factory workers lived, in the next town. Laurie Baxter, 16 Renfrew Street. Now why in the world should anyone want to bother about Laurie Baxter running in a ten-mile race?

"Who will win, do you think?" asked John. "Laurie Baxter?"

"Good gracious, no," said the secretary. "He'll be about halfway. He's not much good."

"Oh well – thank you very much," said John and went out. Now, was he right or wasn't he, in thinking that Laurie Baxter was the number 62 that the man in the wood was

telling the other fellow about, for some reason
or another? And was he right in thinking that
the fellow in hiding was going to lie in wait for
Laurie Baxter? If only he knew!

He couldn't possibly go to the police and
say "I think that Laurie Baxter will probably
disappear halfway through tomorrow's race,
and not turn up at the end because somebody
in Oaktree Wood is lying in wait for him!" It
sounded too silly for words – and it might not
be true. It was only what John thought, not
what he knew. He wondered what to do. Then
he decided that he, too, would hide at the edge
of Oaktree Wood, just before the race, and he
would see if anything happened. He could
always give the alarm if an attack was made on
number 62.

So, the next afternoon, feeling rather
excited, John made his way to Oaktree Wood.
He chose a tree that overlooked the stretch
of road that ran by the wood, down which the
runners would go, and he climbed it, making
sure that there was nobody to see him.

Then he sat on a branch and waited. After a
long, long time the first runner appeared. He
was number 7. Apparently they were not
running in their right order, but just anyhow,
each starting off two minutes after the last.

Then number 16 appeared, and after him number 43. Then came 1 and 8 and 17, each some time after the other. Would 62 never come?

Then came one that looked like 62 but when he got nearer John saw that he was 63. Blow! Three or four more came – and then, surely, surely this was 62?

It was! He was a weedy youth, not a very good runner, with thin shoulders and skinny legs. He came along the road to a curve. And then things happened.

Somebody shot out from the hedge, clamped strong arms round Laurie and dragged him swiftly back into the undergrowth. His hand was over Laurie's mouth. John gasped. It was all so sudden. He caught a glimpse of a second man, and then Laurie was bundled away so quickly that except for a swishing of branches as the men forced their way into the undergrowth, there was nothing to be seen or heard.

John quickly shinned down the tree. He ran after the men but they had disappeared. Then, in the distance, he heard the sound of a car being started up. Oh, so the men had a car hidden somewhere in a glade, had they? If only he could see it and take its number!

But by the time he got to the little clearing, the car was moving away, and all that John could see was that it was red. Red! Then probably it was the same car he had seen the man in the day before. He had got part of the number of the car, but not all of it. Blow!

The car came to a road in the wood and soon the sound of its engine died away in the distance. John sat down on an old tree-trunk to think. Now he wished he had gone to the police and reported what he had thought might happen. It had happened. He didn't know why, or what the men were after – but the thing was, Laurie Baxter had been attacked and taken away in a car. He'd better go to the police and tell them about that.

So off he went. He marched into the station and asked to speak to the sergeant, who was a friend of his uncle's. Then he told him what he knew.

"Please, sir, Laurie Baxter, number 62 of the ten-mile runners, was attacked and taken off in a car, just as he was running beside Oaktree Wood," said John. "I saw it happen. I was up in a tree, waiting for it to happen, as a matter of fact."

"Waiting for it to happen?" said the sergeant, surprised. "What do you mean? How did you know it would happen?"

John told him everything – how he had overheard "number 62" in the wood, said by the man from the car – how he had looked at all houses that might be the number 62 meant – and then how he had thought it must be the number 62 of the runners.

"And it was," said John. "I wonder why Laurie Baxter was attacked, though."

"I don't," said the sergeant, grimly. "I have an idea that he was in a burglary committed three weeks ago, and that he got off with most of the goods and sold them – while the others got nothing! Something scared them in the middle of the robbery and two of them fled, but Laurie apparently didn't. He waited, then when all was quiet he took the goods and made off. I reckon the other fellows are angry with him and want to know what he's done with their share."

"Oh," said John. "But why didn't you arrest Laurie Baxter then, if you knew all this?"

"We questioned him, and put a watch on him," said the sergeant, "but we thought if we let him go free the others might make contact with him and then we'd pull in the whole lot. But now it looks as if we've lost them all."

"Well, sir – I managed to get part of the number of their car," said John, eagerly. "Look – L39 . . . ST. The car was red, sir, and was a sports saloon."

"Good boy!" said the sergeant, and took John's notebook. "This will help tremendously. We can stop all cars of this description."

Then a radio call at once went out to police patrols. "Calling all cars, calling all cars. Please

watch for a red car, make unknown, sports saloon type, registration L39, middle unknown, ends with letters ST. Three men inside. Hold for questioning. Over."

"Can I stay here and see if anything happens, please?" asked John, excited.

"Right," said the sergeant. "Seeing that you've brought us so much information, you can wait – I might want to ask you more questions, mightn't I?"

So John waited. He had a cup of tea with the sergeant and felt very important. Many telephone calls came in, but nothing exciting, until at last there came the one the sergeant wanted. He turned to John.

"They've got them! The car was stopped at Reading. The registration number is L392 BST. It's a red Ford sports saloon. Three men inside, one of them Laurie Baxter. *Now* we'll get going!"

They did. Laurie was so angry with his companions for attacking and kidnapping him that he gave the whole show away. He told where the rest of the unsold stolen goods were, and related his companions share in the various robberies they had committed together.

"So now," finished the sergeant, smiling at the excited boy in front of him, "they'll all spend a nice quiet little time thinking over their sins in prison. They'll commit no more robberies for a while – thanks to you, Detective John!"

And Detective John went proudly home. He'd solved another problem. Now – what would the next one be?

Caravan
Holiday

"Aren't we going to have a summer holiday this year?" Geoffrey asked, gloomily. "Nobody's mentioned one."

"Don't be a selfish little beast," said Ann, his younger sister. "You know Mummy's been terribly ill and Daddy's spent loads of money on her. We can't possibly mention summer holidays."

"No, we can't," said her older sister, Jenny. "All the same – we could do with one after all our worry and anxiety."

"Quite right," said Roddy, looking up from his book. He was eighteen, and kept all the others in order. "We *could* do with one. And we're going to have one. I've managed it."

"Oh, Roddy! You never said a word!"

"Well, I've only just arranged it," said Roddy. "Dad's said I can borrow the small car – and I've borrowed a small caravan from a friend of mine – and I thought we'd go caravanning for two weeks."

163

"Gosh! How super!"

"Roddy! What made you think of it?"

"I'd rather do that than anything in the world!"

Roddy grinned. "I thought you'd like it. Geoff and I can sleep in a tent each night, and you two girls can bunk in the caravan."

"It'll be great," sighed Jenny.

"That depends," said Roddy. "Caravanning isn't the same as going to stay at a hotel, you know, where all your beds are made for you, your meals cooked and everything done. We shall have to do everything ourselves."

"I can't cook," said Jenny. "I don't like that sort of thing. I'm no good at it."

"Well, you'll have to try your hand at it," said Roddy. "We'll all have our jobs. Mine will be the car and looking after it. Geoff's will be all the odd jobs of getting wood for the fire, putting up the tent, and that kind of thing. Do you good, Geoff. You're too lazy for words."

Geoffrey was lazy. He wouldn't do a thing for anyone unless he had to. But he was so excited about the idea of going off in a caravan that he was ready to promise anything.

"You and Ann will have to do the shopping, cleaning and cooking," said Roddy. "And I hope Ann gets over her fear of cows, horses, earwigs, bats, snakes, moths and caterpillars, as we are quite likely to meet a good many of them on our way."

Ann shivered. She was very silly about things like that. But she was not going to give up this holiday lightly. Perhaps they wouldn't meet so many of those awful things as Roddy thought.

"And before we go, one thing's to be quite understood," said Roddy. "My word's law, see! You all toe the line on this holiday, and nobody shirks or messes about. We've got to pull together if we're going to enjoy ourselves. And if you play any monkey tricks, young Geoff, I'll kick you out," said Roddy, still in a very friendly tone, but with a hint of sternness behind it that made Geoff remember how he had forgotten to clean his bicycle the week before, and had lost Roddy's knife only yesterday.

They all began to talk at once. What clothes to take, where they would go, how to manage about camping each night.

"I've got a campers' guide," said Roddy, pulling it out. "It gives all the fields we are allowed to camp in, and which farmer to go to about it, and the rules you have to keep. No leaving field gates open for cattle or horses to stray out of, you know. Things like that."

They all read the little guide eagerly. They decided to strike out across country, keeping close to farms, so that they could buy food easily.

"Will the car be able to pull a heavy caravan?" asked Geoff.

Roddy nodded. "Oh yes – easily. It's not one of those monster caravans, you know. It's arriving tomorrow."

Sure enough it did. The children rushed to the drive to watch it being towed in. It was painted blue and yellow, and was quite modern. They opened the door and went inside.

"A sink! With taps to turn! Where does the water come from – a tank in the roof?"

"Look at all the cups and plates and things. And it's even got a cooking stove."

"Look at these bunks. They fold up flat in the daytime. They look jolly comfortable."

"Bags I the top one."

They were all delighted with it. They wished their mother and father were there too, but they had gone away. Their mother was convalescing now, and the children had been left in the charge of old Hannah, the cook-housekeeper, and Roddy.

Hannah spoilt them and Roddy didn't. Roddy was quite determined to take his father's place and keep them in order. Lazy Geoff, fussy Jenny, and timid Ann were all in awe of their big brother.

"We're starting off tomorrow, don't forget," said Roddy to Jenny. "See that everything is packed into the caravan – all the things we'll need, I mean. Hannah will help you. You ought to be able to manage that."

"Well, Ann must help," said Jenny, who hated jobs of this sort. She had made up her mind she was going to be an actress when she was grown up, very beautiful, very much sought-after and spoilt. She didn't mean to do all the things her mother did so well. She wasn't going to bother about dull things like mending and making beds, cooking, cleaning and washing. Let somebody else do those!

Ann and Jenny set to work to pack, though actually Hannah did most of it. Geoff was sent to clean the outside of the caravan. It was beautifully clean inside but had got splashed with mud during a rain-storm on the way. Roddy went to fill the car up with petrol and oil, and to pump the tyres up, too.

They were all ready to start out the next day. Hannah waved goodbye, thinking with relief that now she really *could* get on with a bit of cleaning. The car started up with Roddy driving it and Geoff sitting beside him.

The girls were looking out of the back windows, waving to Hannah. The sun shone down brilliantly. It was going to be very, very hot.

"Here we go!" said Roddy, and the car started moving. The caravan jerked and followed. Down the drive they went, the caravan running docilely after the car.

"Goodbye, Hannah!" shrieked Jenny. "We're off! We're going to have a simply wonderful time!"

Soon they were several miles on their way.

The sun was now very hot. They went on until they came to the place where they had decided to have their lunch. It was at the top of a hill, and there was a magnificent view from where they sat, munching sandwiches hungrily.

"This is lovely," said Geoff, lying down on his back. "I wish I could eat some more. But I can't. I feel like a nap."

"Well, pick up your sandwich bag first, you lazy kid," said Roddy. "Don't leave litter about."

"Can't just now," said Geoff, sleepily. "Will in a minute."

Roddy said no more. Geoff's sandwich wrapper did a little dance in the wind and then flew off down the hill. Roddy didn't do anything to stop it. Ann took a look at his face and grinned. She knew what that look meant!

"Half an hour's rest and we'll go on," announced Roddy, taking out a book from his pocket. The girls wandered off and Geoff did a little light snoring.

When the girls appeared again Roddy poked Geoff with his foot. "Wake up, Geoff. Pick up your rubbish, and come to the car. Hurry up!"

Geoff sat up and looked round. "Where is it?" he asked. "Can't see any rubbish."

"Down there," said Roddy, pointing far down

the hill. "Come on! If you'd picked it up when you were told to, you wouldn't have had to go miles after it."

"Well, I'm not going to climb all the way down there this hot afternoon," said Geoff, indignantly.

"Don't, then. But you're not getting into the car till you've picked it up," said Roddy. "I'll give you ten minutes."

So Geoff sulkily climbed down to fetch the sandwich wrapper, and grew very hot indeed clambering back. Roddy grinned at him. "Your own fault, old boy," he said. "One of the rules of caravanners and campers, you know – leave no litter."

They set off again. It was a lovely ride. The sun shone down, hotter than ever, but there was always a breeze blowing and Roddy had the sunshine roof open.

They missed out tea because they had had such an enormous lunch. They drove on and on for miles, passing through tiny villages, bigger towns, going up and down hills, and over bridges.

Then at last they came to where they were to camp for the night. It was a big field with a small clear stream running by one end of it. Cows stood not far off, chewing the cud.

Ann gave a scream. "Not here, Roddy! There are cows!"

"So there are. Good. We can get some milk from the farm in the morning," said Roddy, stepping out of the car. "I'm just going to arrange things with the farmer. Geoff, get a fire going please, to cook a meal. You know how to. You'll find plenty of twigs in that little wood over there. Ann, you and Jenny get a meal ready. Some bacon and tomatoes would be nice. There's a frying-pan in the caravan."

He went off, paying no attention to Ann's wailing. "But I'm afraid of the cows, Roddy, I can't stay here for the night. You know how I hate cows."

"Well, they must hate you too coming into their field and yowling about them like that," said Geoff, in disgust. "I'm going to get some sticks for the fire. You'd better stay in the caravan, Ann, in case one of the cows comes over to see what you're making a fuss about. If I were a cow I'd stick my horns in you and toss you over the hedge."

"You're a hateful boy," wailed Ann. She went into the caravan and would not stir out of it at all. Jenny was cross.

"You might help me," she grumbled. "You know I'm not much good at cooking. Oh, blow – where did we put the bacon?"

She got everything ready and Ann gave her a little help, though she would not come out of the caravan. But when Jenny was ready with the frying-pan, the bacon and the tomatoes, there was no fire!

"Geoff! Geoff! Where are you? You haven't made the fire, you lazy thing!" she yelled.

Geoff was nowhere to be seen. He had gone to the wood to get firewood and had suddenly seen a very large rabbit staring at him. It bolted off a little way then sat up and stared at him again. Geoff believed he might catch it if only he could get near enough. It seemed so very tame.

He forgot all about the firewood. So, when Roddy came back, carrying a pint of milk, some new-laid eggs and a little butter, there was no sign of a meal. He was feeling tired and hungry, and he looked at Jenny in exasperation.

"Well, I did expect you'd have the meal ready."

"It's Geoff. He went off for the firewood and hasn't come back," said Jenny.

"Well, why didn't you send Ann for some?" said Roddy. "Where is she?"

"In the caravan. She won't come out because of the cows," said Jenny.

"Right," said Roddy. "She can stay there."

He went to a copse of nearby trees and brought back some twigs and soon had a fire going. Jenny put some bacon and tomatoes into the pan.

173

"Wait – we shan't need all that," said Roddy. "Geoff's not here and Ann's not coming. Just cook enough for two."

Ann heard him. "I'm hungry, too!" she called. "I want some bacon."

"Well, are you going to come out here and have it then?" said Roddy. "If not, you won't get any. What a baby! Frightened of cows indeed! You're just putting it on."

Bacon and tomatoes and bread were fried for two people. Then Roddy poured out mugs of creamy milk. He and Jenny ate a delicious meal, listening to a yellowhammer somewhere that kept saying "Little bit of bread and no cheese."

Ann peered out of the caravan. She was so hungry that she thought she would brave the cows after all. "I'm coming," she said. "Cook me some supper."

"Cook it yourself!" said Jenny. "I'm not going to start all over again for you, Ann."

"Nice polite family we are," said Roddy. "Well, they say there's nothing like a caravan holiday to knock the rough corners off people."

Ann looked at the fire. It was almost out. She would have to find sticks and make it all over again. She couldn't be bothered. Besides, she would have to go near the cows to get sticks. So she had some bread and butter and milk, and made that do.

"Now, you two go and wash the things in the stream," said Roddy. "Hello, here's Geoff!"

Geoff came along carrying an armful of wood. "I say," he called as he came near. "I've been stalking the tamest rabbit you ever saw. Nearly caught it too. Hope I haven't kept you waiting for the wood."

"Well, you have," said Jenny, indignantly. "We waited ages. We've had our supper. There's no bacon or tomatoes for you because Roddy wouldn't let me cook any. You can have bread and butter and milk."

"But I'm very hungry . . ." began Geoff,

crossly. He glanced at Roddy's face and decided to say no more. He cut himself some bread and butter, and took a raw tomato.

"Come on, Ann – let's wash up," said Jenny with a yawn. "I don't know why I feel so sleepy, but I do. It'll be fun to get into those comfy bunks and go to sleep with the owls hooting around."

"I don't like owls," said Ann. "And if you don't mind, Jenny, I'm going back into the caravan. Those cows have come a bit nearer."

"You'll go and help with the washing-up, or I'll put you on the train tomorrow morning and send you back to Hannah," Roddy said suddenly. Ann stared at the cows and then at Roddy. She decided she was much more scared of Roddy. It would be terrible to go back home before the holiday had properly begun. So, pulling a long face, she walked over the grass with Jenny, keeping as far away from the cows as she could.

They washed the things in the stream. "Isn't Roddy strict?" said Ann. "I hope he's not going to be like this all the time. Oh, look at that cow. It's coming over here, I know it is!"

She fled back to the caravan. Jenny followed, grinning, carrying the washed crockery. The boys were putting up their tent. Roddy was showing Geoff exactly how to do it.

"And you've got to do exactly as I've shown you, or you'll have the tent down on top of us another night," said Roddy. "This will be your job in future, Geoff – putting up the tent at night and taking it down when we leave in the morning."

"We're going to bed, Roddy," said Jenny, with a yawn. "Do you mind? I'm sleepy."

"No, you turn in," said Roddy. "And you'd better turn in too, Geoff. Put the sleeping-bags in the tent – groundsheets first, of course. That's right. I'm going for a bit of a stroll. I won't wake any of you if you're asleep. If you're too hot at night, Jenny, leave the cara-van door open."

"Oh no – the cows might walk in!" cried Ann.

It was fun going to bed in the caravan. The

girls let down the two bunks and arranged
the bedclothes. They washed at the little sink,
and were delighted to get into their pyjamas
and snuggle down into the bunks.

Ann had the top one. At the foot of it was
one of the caravan windows. Ann opened it
to let air into the caravan, because it was very
hot.

"Oh, let's have the door open too," said
Jenny, and swung it wide open. A breath of
sweet-smelling air came in.

"No, Jenny. I simply won't have it open,"
said Ann at once. "Honestly, the cows might
walk in."

"What – up the steps?" cried Jenny. "Don't
be so silly."

But Ann made such a terrible fuss that in
the end Jenny shut the door, grumbling hard.
Ann peeped out of the open window by her
bunk. She saw Geoffrey standing at the tent-
opening in his pyjamas, and called goodnight
to him.

"I'm just going to get into my sleeping-bag!"
he said. "All nice and cosy. Roddy's not back
yet, but he won't be long."

Soon the two girls were almost asleep. It
was nice to hear the gurgle of the stream in the
twilight. A bird gave a sudden little song. It

was a late robin. Then there was only the stream, and the wind in the trees to be heard. The girls fell asleep.

They didn't hear Roddy come back, and get into his sleeping-bag. They didn't hear the sleepy voice of Geoff talking to Roddy for a while.

They heard nothing at all – until Ann awoke with a jump.

She knew where she was at once – in the caravan, of course. How lovely! Then suddenly something bumped against it and shook it. What could it be? Ann sat up and leaned over to the window to look out.

Something was looking in! Ann saw an enormous face and smelled a hot, sweet breath. She screamed at the top of her voice and everyone woke up.

"Help! Help! Something's come to get me!" yelled Ann, and stared in horror at the face still looking in at the window. It was not a very dark night, but dark enough for Ann not to be able to see exactly what it was and light enough for her to make out two big, staring eyes.

"What is it, Ann?" cried Jenny, sitting up. Ann went on screaming. Roddy and Geoff came rushing into the caravan, scared stiff.

Whatever was happening to the girls?

"Look – look – something's come to get me!" screamed Ann. "Make it go away! Kill it, Roddy."

Roddy flashed on his torch. Now the enormous face at the window could be seen clearly. It had a long brown and white nose, big eyes fringed with long eyelashes – and a pair of curving horns.

"Good heavens – it's only a cow," said Roddy in disgust. "Just a cow looking in at the window – and you scream the place down and wake everyone up! I'm ashamed of you, Ann."

The cow backed away towards the ropes of the tent. Geoff ran to shoo it off, afraid that the tent might come down.

"Just find out whether there's something to scream about before you wake us all up again," said Roddy. "No, don't shut the window, Ann, this caravan is like a furnace!"

"I won't have cows breathing all over me through the window," said Ann, in tears.

"Well, I shall leave the door open then," said Jenny. "I'm not going to suffocate in here because of your fear of cows. You can choose whether you'll have cows breathing over you, or cows trying to climb up the steps of the caravan."

"Or you can take my sleeping-bag and a groundsheet and sleep under the caravan," said Roddy, grinning to himself. Ann gave a squeal.

"What – with hedgehogs and earwigs and things running all over me! You beast, Roddy!"

The door remained open. Ann lay listening for cows again, but none came. So she fell asleep and did not disturb anyone again that night.

It was a lovely day when they all woke up at last. Ann awoke first because she heard cows mooing and she sat up in fright, thinking they were in the caravan. But they were at the other end of the field. A little dog was looking in at the door and Ann stared back at him.

Should she squeal and wake Jenny because there was a strange dog there? The little thing looked at her and wagged its tail. And, to her surprise, Ann heard herself saying, "Good little dog, then!"

Whereupon the dog came right into the caravan, saw Jenny's face nearby on the lower bunk and gave it a lick! Jenny woke up suddenly and Ann nearly rolled out of the top bunk, squealing with laughter at the sight of Jenny's astonished face.

"Golly – do you mean to say you're not

scared of this dog!" said Jenny, seeing Ann lean down to pat it. "What's come over you?"

They had breakfast out in the field. Boiled eggs, bread and butter, ripe plums and milk that Geoff had just fetched from the farm. It tasted quite different from exactly the same breakfast at home.

They got ready to set off again. Jenny and Ann washed up the plates, and looked at the map with the boys. "Over the hills and far away!" sang Ann, happily. Then Roddy put his head in at the door of the caravan.

"Just look here!" he said crossly to the girls. "Your bunks aren't made. The caravan isn't tidied up. And Jenny's clothes are all over the place. You're two lazy kids, and we shan't move on till everything is spick and span."

"We can do all that later on," said Jenny sulkily.

"Well, you won't," said Roddy. "I never knew such a putter-off as you, Jenny. I tell you, if you don't play your part properly during this holiday, I'll leave you behind somewhere!"

He went off to show Geoffrey how to fix the car to the caravan. It was quite easy but had to be done carefully. "I could do this each day for you," said Geoff, anxious to be in Roddy's good books.

"Right," said Roddy. "I'll trust you to do that. It's time you had a bit of responsibility. After all, you're not a silly kid any more."

They had a lovely day. When they came to a beautiful old village Roddy stopped at a garage to check the tyre pressures. He thought one wheel had a slow puncture.

"You kids can wander about a bit," he said. "Do you good to stretch your legs. Jenny, don't forget you're responsible for the food side of this holiday. Geoff, here's some money – get me some cigarettes, will you? And Ann, buy some postcards somewhere and send one off to Mum. You know her address."

"We'd do everything without being told so often," said Ann. "You're always telling us to do things."

"If I thought you'd do them without being told, I wouldn't open my mouth," Roddy said, with a grin. "But you wouldn't! Now cut along."

A little way beyond the village was a big field. Hearing curious trumpeting sounds from it, the three children went to explore, Ann a little timidly.

"I say, look – it's a circus camp," said Geoff, thrilled. "Let's come and sit on the fence and watch. We might see something."

"Will there be lions or tigers or bears?"

"Dozens!" said Geoff, wickedly. "And probably crocodiles and enormous snakes, and . . ."

Ann screamed and wouldn't go any nearer. In fact she decided not to look at all when she saw one of the elephants apparently going for a walk by itself round the field. She left the others and went back to the town.

She found some postcards and wrote one to her mother. Then she wandered about by herself, buying some sweets in a little shop.

Soon it was half past twelve – the time Roddy had told them all to be back at the caravan. The others came running up at the same time. Roddy looked pleased. "Good. I quite thought I'd have to sit here for ages tooting my horn for you. Get in."

Up the hills and down, once catching a glimpse of blue sea far away, went the little company of caravanners. They had tea in a tea-shop garden, and ate new-baked bread with honey, and hot scones with jam and cream. They all had enormous appetites, and the waitress had to bring them out a second supply of her scones.

"We'll be at our next stopping-place in nice time," said Roddy, looking at the map. "See – there it is – South Tollington – and we ask for Fenton Farm. There's no stream nearby though – so we can't wash in stream water – we'll have to make do with the caravan water."

They arrived at about seven o'clock. Roddy went off to the farm at once and came back in a few minutes time looking rather annoyed.

"He says we can stay for the night but he won't let us have any milk or anything," said Roddy. "Apparently the last lot of campers stole two or three of his chickens – or so he says – and now he's not going to supply anybody else with anything. Never mind – we must make do with what we've got. What are we going to have for supper, Jenny?"

Jenny suddenly looked dismayed. She stared

at Roddy, going red. "I – I don't know," she said.

"Whatever do you mean – you don't know?" said Roddy. "What did you buy this morning?"

"Well – actually Roddy – you see – what happened – well, you see . . . " began Jenny, going redder than ever.

"Answer me properly," said Roddy.

"I forgot about the shopping," said Jenny. "Geoff and I found a circus in the field – and we went and sat on the fence – and . . ."

"Do you mean to say there's no supper for us!" cried Roddy. "And I can't get anything from the farm either. Well, you really are the limit. Selfish, lazy lot – that's what you are!"

"I did buy some cards and send one to Mummy," said Ann, in rather a small voice. The others rounded on her at once.

"Yes, and why did you? Only because you were scared of looking at the circus camp!"

"Well, I'm going for a stroll," said Roddy, in disgust. "Where are my cigarettes, Geoff? I gave you the money for them this morning."

Now it was Geoff's turn to go red and to stammer. He had forgotten those too! Roddy stared at him in anger, swung on his heel, and went off by himself. The others felt most uncomfortable, but instead of blaming themselves they began to say nasty things about Roddy.

"Always flying into a temper!"

"Expecting us to do every single thing he tells us."

"Blow his beastly cigarettes."

All the same it was distinctly annoying to have no supper because they were all very hungry. The cupboard in the caravan was bare except for a hunk of stale bread and a bit of hard cheese. Jenny looked at it. "We'd better let Roddy have that," she said, and put it on a plate.

"And I'd better put up the tent," said Geoff sulkily. "Get into a row if I don't!"

He put it up carelessly. The girls, feeling hungry and cross, decided to go to bed. There were no cows to worry about tonight, but there was a large spider in a corner of the caravan that made Ann squeal. However, neither Jenny nor Geoff would remove it.

"Squeal away," said Geoff. "Go on till Roddy comes back, if you dare. He's in a mood to box your ears tonight!"

So Ann stopped squealing and got fearfully into her bunk. Geoff got into his sleeping-bag and waited for Roddy. But Roddy was a very, very long time. He had found somewhere to have a meal and he sat there for a long while. What was he to do with his lazy, irresponsible, selfish brother and sisters? He had given up a lovely holiday in Scotland to give the kids a treat – and if this kind of thing was going to happen all the time he was going to wish he had gone to Scotland after all!

He didn't see the plate of bread and cheese when he got back. A mouse discovered it in the night and helped himself. It was a good thing that Ann didn't know that or she would have squealed the place down again! Roddy got into his sleeping-bag, yawned and went to sleep.

The wind got up in the night. The rain came down in squalls. It beat against the caravan and the tent. The wind tugged at the tent and made it flap.

Suddenly something gave way and the tent collapsed completely. It fell over Roddy and

Geoff, waking them up suddenly, smothering them as they tried to push it off them.

"Good heavens! The tent's down!" said Roddy at last. "You silly little idiot, Geoff – I suppose you put it up carelessly as I wasn't there to watch you. Now we'll have to mess about in the dark and the rain for ages!"

The two boys had a very difficult time with the collapsed tent. Roddy made Geoff work

hard for he knew it was his fault. Geoff knew that too. It would have been all right if only this wind hadn't got up! Cold, wet through, and cross, the boys were at last able to get into their sleeping-bags again and settle down in the newly-put-up tent. Geoff was sulky and would not apologise. Roddy was angry.

"I had to go off and find a meal for myself tonight," he began, "and I've a good mind to go off and find a bed for myself too. Not one of you does his or her bit . . ."

"How mean of you – getting supper for yourself and forgetting all about us!" Geoff said angrily, feeling hungrier than ever.

"I didn't forget you," said Roddy. "You went hungry because it was your own faults – good lesson for you – but I didn't see why I should suffer because of your carelessness and forgetfulness. And what about this tent tonight? What about an apology for your carelessness over that?"

"You won't get one," said Geoff. "I think you're horrid. I really do think it's the limit getting a meal for yourself and –"

"One more word from you and you'll get out of this tent," said Roddy. He meant it. Geoff didn't say another word. He was angry with Roddy – but he was angry with himself too for being careless over putting up the tent.

Nobody was very cheerful in the morning. For one thing Ann, Jenny and Geoff were very hungry and there was nothing to eat till they got to the next town. For another thing there was no water for anyone to wash in! That was Ann's fault! She had left the tap running a little all night long – and now there was no water left in the tank in the roof of the caravan.

"Well, I really don't expect anything else from any of you," said Roddy, sarcastically. "No food – no water – no cigarettes – tent collapsing. There's not much else you can do!"

He went off to tell the farmer they were leaving. "Come and help me fix the caravan to the car, for goodness sake," said Geoff to the others. "I'll get into another row if I don't do it just how he showed me."

"Do it yourself," said Jenny, annoyed. "I've got the caravan to tidy. I shall get into a row if I don't do that. This is a beastly holiday. I hate it. I wish it would end quickly."

Roddy came back, saw that the caravan was fixed to the car, noticed the three sulky faces, and said nothing. He felt sad. They had all looked forward to this holiday – and now, just because they couldn't pull together and each play their part, it was going to be a failure.

They set off. They had a good breakfast in the next town and felt a bit better. They even began to talk cheerfully again. "Where are we going today? What are we going to do?"

"I thought we might head towards the sea now," said Roddy, opening the map. "The weather is so hot we could do with a bit of swimming. We might get permission to put the caravan up on the cliffs somewhere, so that we could get a good view of the sea."

Everyone cheered up considerably. This sounded simply lovely. "Yes, let's go towards the sea," said Jenny. "We've brought swimming costumes with us, luckily."

They set off again. They were all looking out for the first sight of the sea when they came to it. They had pleasant thoughts of bathing in the cool water and basking in the sun to dry.

"Golly! Look at this hill we've got to climb," said Jenny. "Isn't it frightfully steep?"

It was. The car groaned up it. Roddy stopped halfway and made the other three get out. "If we get rid of your weight, maybe the caravan won't be too heavy for the car," he said. He set off again, and the children followed on foot.

And then suddenly something dreadful

193

happened. Geoff had not fixed the caravan properly to the car and the steepness of the hill, making the van drag heavily on the car, broke the fastening between them. The caravan broke away – the car suddenly shot forward, relieved of its weight – and the caravan began to run backwards down the hill all by itself!

"Look! Look!" screamed Ann, suddenly. "The caravan is running backwards. It's broken away from the car! Look out!"

The caravan, looking most peculiar, lumbered down the hill, gathering speed as it went. The frightened children squeezed into the hedge as it passed them, afraid of being knocked down. Strangely enough the caravan kept to the roadway, though it veered occasionally from side to side.

Roddy stopped the car. He jumped out of it in time to see the caravan careering down the hill by itself. He stood in horror, unable to do anything to stop it. He suddenly felt very sick. What if it caused a terrible accident? Suppose another car was coming up the hill?

The caravan turned a corner and disappeared from sight. Roddy waited for the sound of a crash. Ann ran up the hill to him, white-faced and sobbing.

"Roddy! Roddy! The caravan's gone. Oh, Roddy!"

The others joined Roddy too, pale and frightened. "Oh, Roddy," said Geoff, his mouth quivering, "it was my fault I know. I didn't fix it properly."

They all sat down, feeling very shaky at the knees. Roddy put his arm round Ann, who was almost sick with fright.

"It's a dreadful thing," he said, in a quiet voice. "I – I hardly like to go down the hill and see what's happened. The least we can hope for is that the caravan has smashed itself – without smashing any other car or hurting anyone."

"I wished for this holiday to come to an end – but I didn't mean it to be like this," wept Jenny. "Oh, Roddy, it's awful. Will we have to pay for the caravan?"

"Of course – and for any damage it has done too," said Roddy, looking as white as the others. "I ought to have looked to see that Geoff had fixed it properly. It's my fault too. Perhaps I've tried to make you do too many things – in the wrong way. Well, this is a terrible punishment for not being able to pull together."

"Don't say things like that!" cried Jenny. "And don't look like that, Roddy. We've been awful. We haven't helped you a bit. Oh, I wish we could begin all over again, and do better."

"Well, we can't," said Roddy, getting up. "The holiday is finished. The caravan is smashed to pieces. Come on – we'll have to go and face it sometime."

In silence they went down the hill. Round the corner they went, afraid of what they might see. There was no sign of the caravan at all. They went on, looking fearfully from side to side. But there was no caravan to be seen.

They met an old man. "Have you seen our caravan running away?" asked Roddy.

The old man looked most astonished and shook his head. "I ain't seen no caravan at all," he said. "You didn't ought to let one run away. Them's not safe things running about on their own."

The children would have smiled at this any other time. But they couldn't now. They hurried on, afraid of what they might see at any moment.

Soon they came to a gap in the hedge. It looked as if something had broken through. They looked over the hedge and saw a most extraordinary sight!

There, standing in the field, was their caravan, surrounded by a circle of staring cows. It did not appear to be damaged at all. There it was, gleaming blue and yellow, standing by a little stream. They ran to it in excitement. They went all round it, their faces glowing.

"Roddy! It's not damaged at all! Not even a scratch, except just here where the thorns in the hedge caught it!"

"Oh, Roddy – it's too good to be true!"

"I can't believe it! Not a thing wrong with it!"

Ann was so delighted to see the caravan, whole and undamaged, that she took no notice of the cows at all. She slipped her arm through Roddy's.

"Oh, Roddy – aren't you glad? Our holiday hasn't ended after all!"

Roddy pulled the others down on to a bank

and looked at them gravely. "Well," he said, "it's a miracle the caravan is all right and that it hasn't smashed into anything or hurt anyone. But I think, kids, our holiday is at an end, anyhow. This is a terrible lesson to us. Because we didn't all play our parts and pull together as we should have done, this happened. We had better go home before anything worse comes."

Geoff looked at Roddy. "Nothing worse will come, Roddy. Don't break up this holiday. I'll play my part in future. You can trust me absolutely."

"And me too," said Jenny. "I'm sorry for all my temper and forgetfulness. Honestly, I'll do my bit. I feel so very, very thankful that nothing terrible has happened after all."

"I do too," said Ann. "I won't be silly or fuss any more. I won't even scream when I see a spider. I'll do everything you want me to, Roddy. But do, do let's go on with the holiday. We'll all pull together now."

Roddy smiled his nicest smile. "All right," he said. "We'll go on. I hoped you'd all want to. I do, too. We'll have a perfectly splendid time now – lovely meals from Jenny, no more squeals from Ann, plenty of good work from Geoff. And I'll keep my temper and think you're all perfectly wonderful!"

He got up. "We'd better see to the caravan now," he said. "We'll want a bit of help getting it out of this field. Then off we'll go again and make our way towards the sea!"

Two men helped them to get the caravan on the road once more. Roddy ran the car down to it and fixed the two together properly. They all got in.

"Now, off we go," said Roddy. "And this time we'll really enjoy ourselves!"

The
Lost Treasure

James, Susie and George were all feeling very sad. Not so much because they were going back to their boarding-schools in a few days, but because when they next broke up for the holidays, their lovely home, Grey Towers, would belong to someone else!

"Why can't we keep it for ourselves?" asked Susie. "Mummy, it's been our home, and Daddy's home, and Grandpa's home, and even Great-grandpa's home! Why have we got to leave? It ought to be our home too!"

"Well, dear, we're not so well off now," said her mother. "We can't afford to keep up a big place like this, even though it has belonged to us for three hundred years! Our family used to be rich, you know, in your great-great-grandfather's time. But then he offended a friend of the king and he was stripped of all his money and the famous family jewels."

"*All* of them?" said James, who had heard this story before. "I thought that Great-great-grandpa hid some of his treasure."

"So the tale goes," said Mother. "But I'm afraid I don't believe that now, James. It would have been found long ago if it had been hidden. Anyway, dozens of our family have looked for it and haven't found it."

"I've looked for it too," said George, the eldest. "I've looked everywhere. I thought there might be a secret panel or something somewhere, which led to a hidden cupboard, but I never found anything."

"And all because long ago one of our family offended somebody, we've got to leave the home we love, and go and live somewhere we'll hate," said James.

"I do so love Grey Towers," said Susie. "Mummy, I can't bear to think I'll never come home to it again. I shall go and say goodbye to every single bit of it before I go back to school."

"Yes, we'd better do that," said James. "We'll go into every room and every corner so that we'll remember it always. Let's start now. Let's go up to the towers and look out of the windows, so that we can see all the country around that we know so well."

"Yes. And we'll even go down to the cellars and say goodbye to those," said George. "Not that I've ever been very fond of them, but I'm

not going to miss anything!"

"Well, we'll take Jumpy with us then," said Susie. "There might be rats there and I don't like them. Jumpy can chase them for us. He's a good dog for rats."

They began to say goodbye for the last time to all the places they loved so well – the rounded tower rooms at each end of the house – their own bedrooms, tucked into the roof – their big games room with its magnificent view of the nearby sea – the long dark landing where they had often hidden to pounce at one another.

"We mustn't leave out anything," said Susie, dolefully. "We'll do the cellars last. Where's Jumpy?"

"Jumpy!" called George, when at last they were ready to go down into the dark cellars. "Jumpy! Come along! We want you to come down and chase rats! Rats, boy, RATS!"

"And that's about all we shall find down in those old cellars," said Susie with a shiver. And down the stone steps they went, with Jumpy leaping beside them.

The cellars were deep down under the house. They were dark and smelled damp and musty. There was no electric light there so the children had torches. Jumpy didn't mind the dark at all. He rushed here and there, sniffing in every corner for rats.

Old barrels lined the walls. Empty bottles, thick with dust and cobwebs, stood on dark shelves. Wooden crates stood about. It was not a very pleasant place.

There were three or four cellars of different sizes. Nothing of any value was kept there now because Mother said it was too damp to store things. So it wasn't really a very interesting place after all.

"I don't feel I mind saying goodbye to the cellars, really," said Susie, flashing her torch round. "I never liked them much. Ugh, is that a frog?"

"No – a rat! Hi, Jumpy, here's a rat for you. Rat, quick!" yelled George. Jumpy raced up at once, his tail quivering in delight. The rat shot

into the next cellar and Jumpy tore after him. The children followed with their torches.

The rat ran round the cellar, looking for a way of escape, but there was none there. It went into the last cellar of all, a place so hung with cobwebs that Susie stopped in dismay, feeling the webby fingers across her face.

"It's horrid here!" she said. "I won't go in!"

Jumpy chased the rat to a corner, where a big barrel stood. Then he scraped and whined loudly, trying to get beneath the barrel.

"The rat's found a way out somehow," said James, in disgust. "I wonder if it could have gone under this barrel. Help me to overturn it, George. That's right – over it goes! There, Jumpy, is the rat under it?"

No, it wasn't. But there was a dark hole there and Jumpy suddenly fell down it unexpectedly, disappearing with a loud yelp!

"Gracious! What's happened to Jumpy?" said Susie, in alarm. The boys shone their torches on the floor under the barrel they had overturned.

"There's a round hole there! Where does it lead to?" said George. "Look, it's had a wooden lid or something over it at one time but it's rotted away. What a funny thing! Jumpy! Are you all right?"

A doleful wail came up. Jumpy was plainly not at all happy. He was very frightened. The boys shone their torches down the hole.

Far down they could see two green eyes gleaming up at them. It was poor Jumpy, looking up in despair.

"We'll get a rope and go down and get Jumpy up," said George. "What a funny pit. What can it be for? We'll go down and see, shall we? Maybe it was just a hiding-place for a smuggler!"

"Yes, that's it," said James. "We know that smuggling was carried on here ages ago. Fancy us never finding this old hole before. Come on – let's get a rope and rescue poor old Jumpy. What a noise he's making."

Soon the three children had found a rope and were back in the dark cellars. Jumpy was still howling mournfully, and the echoes of his doleful voice filled the cellars and made Susie shiver.

"I don't like it," she said. "Let's rescue Jumpy quickly and get back into the daylight again!"

"I'd better go down on the rope and tie Jumpy to it, and you must haul him up somehow," said George. "Then I'll come up on the rope myself. It's not very far down – less

than three metres, I should think."

He let the rope down after first tying it firmly to an iron hook in the wall. Then down he went, hand over hand, to poor Jumpy. The dog was thrilled to see him and barked joyfully.

George stood at the bottom of the hole, and felt for Jumpy's collar. He meant to tie the rope round his body in such a way that the others could haul him up without hurting him.

He switched on his torch – and then he gave a loud cry that made the others jump. "Look! It isn't just a hole. There's an opening here – it must lead into a passage. Gracious, how exciting!"

James and Susie almost fell down the hole in their excitement. What! An opening out of the hole? Where *could* it lead to?

"I'm coming down too!" shouted James and down he went, landing almost on top of George. Jumpy, happy now that the children were with him, had pranced out through the opening at the bottom. George shouted up to Susie.

"Wait a bit before you come down. Let me and James get into the opening or you'll land on top of us. I'll shout when we're ready."

Susie waited till he shouted. Then down she

went on the rope too, hand over hand, as she had been taught to do at gym.

She saw a small opening at one side of the wall of the hole. She had to bend down to get through it. The two boys were there, waiting, their torches switched on.

"It's a passage!" James said excitedly. "See? There it goes, down and down! Shall we explore it?"

"Well, of course!" said George. "What do you think? I'll go first. Let me squeeze by you. Golly, isn't it narrow!"

"Now Jumpy's gone again," said James. "He must be halfway down the passage by now. Jumpy! Come back, you silly, or you'll get lost."

A distant bark answered him. Jumpy was doing a bit of exploring himself. The children followed, their heads bumping into the rocky roof of the passage every now and again.

"It's leading towards the sea," cried James. "It'll come out somewhere on the shore, I bet it will!"

The passage went down and down, sometimes so steep and rocky that the children almost fell. It was all very strange and exciting. Their torches made patches of light in the darkness, and now and again they caught sight of Jumpy's wagging tail some way in front of them.

James suddenly heard a curious noise. He stopped. "Listen," he said in alarm. "What's that? Can you hear that booming sound? Whatever can it be?"

"I know!" said Susie. "It's the sea! We're coming near the sea."

"I wonder what part of the beach we shall come out on. Won't anyone walking on the beach be surprised to see us!"

Suddenly the steep little passage came to an end. In front of them the children saw a huge wooden door, studded with nails, fitting roughly into a rocky archway.

"A door!" said George. "Fancy finding a door down here! Is it locked?"

It wasn't locked – but it was bolted. Luckily the bolts were on their side of the door. With Jumpy watching impatiently, George and James tried their best to push back the heavy bolts. They couldn't – but the screws that held the bolts to the door suddenly gave way, for they were set in wood that had rotted and grown weak with the years. They fell out and the door swung open before them.

They flashed their torches beyond it. They saw a cave there, a surprisingly large one, with a high rocky roof and a smooth sandy floor. Directly opposite was a tiny opening, just big enough for a man to creep through, that looked out on the sea just below! It was a most astonishing sight.

Daylight came in through the hole in the cave wall. The children switched off their torches and looked round.

"Old trunks! Brass-bound boxes!" cried James running to where they stood in untidy heaps here and there. "Look, Susie, look, George! Do you suppose they'll be empty?"

"Of course," said George. He looked round the cave. "This must have been one of the old smugglers' caves," he said. "A well-hidden one too. You can only get into it from the seaward side by that hole there. The smugglers would have to unpack their goods on the moonlit shore and carry them to that hole, and hand them in to someone waiting in this cave."

"But George – how did these boxes and trunks get here?" asked Susie, looking at them. "If they didn't come from the shore they must have come from our house, Grey Towers, years and years ago!"

"Susie's right! They may have belonged to Grey Towers!" shouted James, and he flung himself down by one of the boxes. "Quick,

let's open them and see what's in them. Oh, quick, quick, quick!"

The children couldn't open the boxes. They must be locked! They were bitterly disappointed. But then, lying half buried in the sand nearby, George suddenly spied an old bunch of keys!

"We'll try these!" he cried, and was soon busy fitting key after key into one of the trunks. Suddenly one key turned with a

grating noise – and George flung open the lid.
Packed hurriedly inside, flung in anyhow, were
all kinds of jewels! Even now, after all the
years of hiding, they gleamed brightly.

"Oh – look!" said Susie, in an awed voice,
and held up what she felt sure must be an

emerald and diamond necklace. "And look at this – it's like a dog-collar made of rubies. And this – and this!"

"It's the old lost treasure of Grey Towers!" said George, and he looked very solemn and yet very excited. "The treasure our great-great-grandfather must have hidden when he was in disgrace with the king. And somehow nobody can have known where he hid it, and when he was taken away and imprisoned and killed, the treasure stayed here and was never, never found – because nobody ever knew about that little round hole in the cellar under the big barrel!"

After this long speech all the children sat silent, thoughts spinning round in their heads. "We shan't need to leave our dear old home now! We can stay on at Grey Towers! We can sell all these things and be rich!"

"But will it be treasure-trove? Will the Queen have to have it?" asked Susie, suddenly.

"Of course not. It's our family's riches, even though they've been lost for years!" said George. "Goodness – what will Mother say?"

"Look what's in this box – old gold pieces!" said James, unlocking another treasure hoard. "What a lovely sound they make when I run my hand through them! Let's fill our pockets

with this money, and dress ourselves up in all the shining jewels, and go and find Mum and Dad! What a surprise we'll give them!"

This seemed a lovely trick to play, and a fine way to show off their discovery. Quickly the children decked themselves out in heavy necklaces, bracelets, brooches, pins and sparkling belts. They filled their pockets with the money, and took some in their hands to fling down before their parents!

"Let's put that collar of rubies on Jumpy," cried George and, giggling with excitement, they did so. Jumpy was astonished by such a heavy collar, but he didn't seem to mind.

Then off they went up the secret passage to the cellars, shouting and laughing in delight. "Here comes the old lost treasure! Here comes the old lost treasure!" they called.

And you should have seen their parents' faces when they saw three dirty, dusty, gleaming children arriving with a ruby-collared dog, flinging gold pieces about, and shouting at the tops of their voices:

"We shan't leave Grey Towers after all, we shan't, we shan't!"

And, of course, they didn't!

Great-Grandpa's Telescope

Great-grandpa was snoozing in the garden in his deckchair. He woke up suddenly. Now, who was that whispering nearby? Couldn't he even have a nap without those boys pestering him?

He couldn't see anyone and the whispering seemed to have stopped. He was just about to close his eyes again when he caught sight of a movement in the hedge. It was a good thick hedge, where birds nested and sang, and was a good hiding-place for any boy or girl who wanted to be unseen.

He watched the hedge. There – the boughs and brambles moved again. He was sure somebody was there. And he was sure he knew who it was. His great-grandson James, with his friend Malcolm. Always up to something!

He called out sharply. "James? Are you hiding there? Come out at once."

An indignant face looked out of the hedge. "Shh!" said James. "SHH!"

"Shh? What do you mean – shh?" said his

221

great-grandfather, crossly.

"Great-grandpa, don't make a noise," said James, in a low voice. "Malcolm and I are watching a kingfisher sitting on a bough over the stream on the other side of the hedge. You'll frighten him away!"

"Oh. I thought you were up to some joke or other," said Great-grandpa, lowering his voice. "I don't take kindly to being squirted with water pistols or being jumped at and booed. So you're watching birds, are you? Well, I used to do that long ago."

"Oh, blow! The kingfisher's gone," said

James, as a brilliant blue-green bird flew over the garden, crying "tee-tee-tee" at the top of his voice.

The two boys came into the garden. James was bright-eyed and merry, Malcolm was solemn and serious. They were great friends because they both loved birds and liked watching them.

They began to talk to the old man and tell him about the birds they had seen. He listened with interest. "You know quite a lot," he said. "Have you seen the big herons down on the marsh? They're interesting birds to watch."

"Yes. But as soon as we go near them they fly off," said Malcolm. "What we want is a pair of binoculars. We could hide in a hedge then, and look through the glasses and see the birds so clearly that they might be really close to us. But nobody will trust us with binoculars."

"Hmm," said Great-grandpa, "I'm not surprised. Binoculars are expensive and valuable things. You boys are so careless nowadays – you don't take care of things as we used to do when I was a boy. Look at your new bike, now, James – new six months ago, and it might be as old as the hills already, it looks so dirty!"

James went red. "I'll clean it this evening," he said. "I promise you, Great-grandpa. I know I've neglected it, and it's a beauty."

"Well, that's the way I like to hear a lad speak," said Great-grandpa, pleased. "And because I know you'll keep your promise, I'll do something for you."

"What?" asked James, eagerly.

"I'll lend you my old telescope," said Great-grandpa. "It's a poor thing compared with modern binoculars, but it still brings far-away things close – and I'll lend it to you to watch the birds."

"Oh, thanks," said both boys, and James beamed all over his face. "Where is it, Great-grandpa? Can I fetch it now?"

His great-grandfather told him where it was, and he ran to get it. Soon he and Malcolm were taking turns at looking through it.

"Oh, I say – it's cracked or something," said James at last. "Everything we look at seems to be cracked in two!"

Great-grandpa looked through it. "Oh, yes – I forgot it was cracked," he said. "It's this glass bit at the end here. Somebody dropped the telescope once and it got rather cracked. But once you get used to the crack, you don't notice it."

Malcolm put the telescope to his eye. "Great! I can see the church tower as close as anything!" he said. "I can see two sparrows quarrelling on it. I can see a blackbird too, sitting at the top of a hawthorn tree."

"Let *me* see," said James, and took it away. "Wow! Doesn't it bring things close? I can see exactly what clothes are hanging out on Mrs Kaley's line, and that's *ever* so far away."

"Now we shall be able to watch the birds properly," said Malcolm.

"We can hide in the hedge, stick the telescope to our eyes, and see birds half a mile away. We'll have fun!"

"Right," said Great-grandpa. "I'll lend it to you. Mind you, it's a poor thing really, old and cracked and not very powerful. You need first-class binoculars if you want to see things properly. But this will be a help, I'm sure."

It *was* a help. The boys went out bird-watching together and took the telescope with them. They didn't only watch the birds. They sat behind a bush, pushed the telescope through the leaves, and watched the rabbits playing in the evenings. They had to laugh at them, they were so comical – and then the rabbits would run away in fright. But they always came back.

225

Having the telescope made the boys want binoculars more than ever. The crack in the lens was annoying. It got a bit worse and the boys found it difficult to see clearly. But even so the telescope was great fun and brought things so close that they could watch the yellowhammer singing at the top of the bush, the sparrows going in and out of their nests under the eaves of old Mrs Hall's cottage, and even follow the swallows swooping in the air catching flies.

"Last night I heard owls," James said to

Malcolm. "We've never been able to watch owls, have we? It's going to be full moon soon and we could do a spot of owl-watching, if you liked. I'd love to see that big barn owl who screeches round the farm sometimes."

"Right. I'll watch tonight," Malcolm said promptly. "It's my turn to have the telescope."

"All right," said James, wishing he could have it first for night-watching. "Take it. You might see the tawny owl, too – I've heard his lovely hoot sometimes."

But the night was cloudy and dark and Malcolm neither saw nor heard any owls. It was most disappointing. He wanted to have the telescope for the second night but James wouldn't let him. "No, it's my turn," he said. "You've got to be fair."

James went to bed as usual that night. He took the telescope with him. He looked at his watch. Half past eight. It wouldn't be time for the owls to come out yet. It was still daylight, for it was high summer.

"I'll set my alarm clock for one o'clock," he thought. "The moon will be out then, and so will all the owls. It will be a good hunting night for them. I'll hear them hooting all over the place – and I bet I'll hear the screech of the old barn owl too."

He went to sleep. At one o'clock his alarm clock woke him up. He had put it under his pillow so that no one else would hear it. He switched off the alarm and sat up. The moon streamed in at his window.

"Ooooooh! Ooo-ooo-ooo-OOOOH!" called a beautiful voice in the night. James nodded. "Tawny owl," he said, pleased. "He's about tonight. Now – I'll train the telescope on to the farmhouse and watch for the barn owl first. Then when I find out where the tawny owl is hooting from, I'll try and see him too."

He saw nothing through the telescope except a big black bat that suddenly flitted across his view and made him jump. But he heard something.

It was a hoot. "Too-whoo, too-whoo, too-whit!" James listened. Then there came an answering call. "Too-whit, too-whit-too-whoo!"

James frowned. What owl was this calling? The hooting didn't sound like any owl he had ever heard! It came again.

Where did it come from? It sounded rather as if it came from somewhere near the old church. James trained the cracked lens of the telescope on to the church and waited for the sight of an owl.

No owl came. No more hoots came either –

but the barn owl suddenly gave one of his harsh shrieks and made James jump. It came from the farmyard. James thought he would train the telescope on to the farmhouse again.

He took one last look at the church tower – and then he stiffened in surprise. Something was moving on the roof of the church. What was it? It wasn't an owl – far too big. Could he be mistaken?

He watched intently. There was no movement for a while, and then he caught sight of another moving shadow on the farther side of the roof. Yes – two black shadows were

there. But they weren't birds – and they couldn't be animals – unless perhaps it was cats! Certainly it couldn't be human beings.

"It must be cats!" thought James, watching through the telescope. "No – it isn't! It's men – two men! They have come right out into the moonlight now and I can see them plainly. But what are men doing on the church roof in the middle of the night?"

He decided to put on some clothes and go next door to Malcolm. He would take the telescope with him.

So, dressing hurriedly, James stole down the stairs and went to the back door. He unlocked it and slipped out. The telescope was safely under his arm. Good gracious! Fancy seeing men on the church roof through it! What a strange thing.

He came to the wall that divided his garden from Malcolm's. Over he went and made his way to the path that ran below Malcolm's window. He picked up a few small pebbles. He took aim and threw one. No good. It fell back again. He threw another and it pinged against the glass pane of the window. He waited a moment, but as nothing happened he threw a third pebble.

That one brought Malcolm to the window!

James heard it being cautiously opened, and called up.

"Malcolm! It's me, James. Come on down. I've got something to tell you. Hurry up!"

"Right," came Malcolm's whisper, and he disappeared. It wasn't long before he was creeping out of his house.

"What is it?" he said to James. "Quick, tell me!"

James clutched hold of Malcolm's arm. He whispered in his ear. "I was watching for owls through the telescope. I heard some peculiar hooting which didn't really sound like owls. It came from near the church, so I trained the telescope on to the church roof, just in case owls were swooping about there."

"Go on," said Malcolm, excited. "Were there any?"

"No. But I saw something moving on the roof," said James. "It wasn't birds, of course – and it wasn't cats, either. It was men!"

"Goodness!" said Malcolm, surprised. "Men? But why should they be wandering about the roof of the church? They must be mad. Did you really see them? Here, give me the telescope."

"You can't see the church roof from down here on the ground," said James. "We'll have to go upstairs if you want to get a view of that.

But don't let's waste time, Malcolm. I want to get along to the church and find out what's going on."

"Yes – you're right. That's the best thing to do!" said Malcolm. "Come on then. Let's keep in the shadows, just in case those men have got a look-out somewhere."

They set off quietly, James with the telescope still tucked under his arm. "I think the hoots I heard were signals made by the men, not by owls," he said. "They didn't sound a bit like owls."

They came near the church. A big yew hedge, dark and thick, ran round the church-yard. The boys crouched behind it, and listened and watched.

At first they heard nothing. Then a slight noise came from the roof of the nearby church. The boys peeped out to look up to it. "There's one man – look!" whispered James, in excitement. "He's carrying something. What is it? It's all very mysterious, isn't it, Malcolm? What can they be doing?"

"What had we better do?" whispered back Malcolm. "I know what I'd like to do!"

"What?" asked James.

"How do you suppose they got up to the roof? By a ladder?" said Malcolm. "Well, *I'd* like to find that ladder and remove it! Then they would be in a great fix, wouldn't they?"

James thought this was a wonderful idea and he said so. "We'd have to make sure that there wasn't a third man or even a fourth hanging about down in the churchyard, keeping watch," he said. "We'd get into awful trouble if they caught us spying on them. Malcolm, let's creep right round the church-yard in the shadow of this yew hedge and listen and look."

So, holding their breath, the two boys made their way slowly and silently round the big churchyard, watching out for any other men that might be there.

Malcolm suddenly clutched James and made him jump. "Quiet!" he hissed in his ear. "Look over there – there's a man – a third man and he's standing at the foot of a ladder, holding it! We can't take it away after all."

"What a pity," said James. They fixed their eyes on the man, who stood with one foot on the long ladder and his two hands holding it. From above came the sounds of panting.

Then a cautious voice spoke from the roof. "You there, Eddie? Come on up for a minute. This piece is too awkward for us to manage between us. We want your help."

"Right," said Eddie, who was a big fellow. He clambered up the ladder and climbed on to the roof. Malcolm gave James a nudge.

"Come on. Now's our chance! We'll remove the ladder, and then you can run for the police while I stay here and watch what happens. We'll have to tug like anything at that ladder. It will be awfully heavy."

The two boys ran to the ladder. They both took hold of it at the bottom and pulled it as hard as they could. The top edge slid down from the roof – lower and still lower – and then the ladder collapsed and fell down to the ground with a very loud noise.

"Quick, hide!" whispered James. "In this doorway here. They won't have seen us. Just see what they say."

They crouched in the doorway and listened. Astonished voices came from the roof high above.

"What was that? The ladder! It's slipped and fallen! Eddie, why didn't you make it secure? Now we can't get down."

"It was safe all right," said Eddie's voice. "Somebody must have pulled it down. Listen!"

There was silence as the men listened. But they heard nothing, for Malcolm and James were as quiet as the church mice!

234

"It slipped," said somebody's voice. "Now what are we going to do? Let's chuck the stuff down and then find a way to climb down ourselves."

"It will make a noise," objected Eddie's voice, but the other men pooh-poohed this.

"It won't make as much noise as that ladder did when it fell! Nobody heard that. The church isn't near the village, and it's the middle of the night. Come on – let's heave this piece over."

There was a heavy thud not far from the two boys, who clutched one another, startled. What in the world were the men stealing and throwing down to the ground?

"I'll run for the police now, before the men get down and run off with their goods," said James. "Keep hidden, Malcolm, won't you?"

James rushed off, keeping in the shadow of the yew hedge again, his feet making no sound. He made his way up the church lane and after a while came to the village. He knew where the police station was. A solitary light burned there. One of the two policemen must be still on duty.

The door was shut but not locked. Malcolm turned the big iron handle and stumbled in. A policeman sitting asleep beside a telephone jumped up in alarm. He was surprised to see James. He knew him quite well.

"What's up?" he said. "What's happened to bring you here at this time of night?"

James poured out his story, and the policeman listened carefully. "But I can't imagine what they're stealing!" said James, out of breath at the end.

"Can't you? I can!" the policeman said grimly. "Our church has a fine lead roof – lead is worth a lot of money now. Those rogues are stripping the roof, meaning to take the sheets of lead away and sell them. And on the first rainy day we'll have the rain pouring into the church and ruining everything."

He made a short telephone call to the other village policeman, who was off duty and asleep at home, and asked him to join them down by the church at once. "Telephone through to headquarters before you leave," said the first policeman. "We'll want a few more men."

Then he set off with the excited James and they went to the churchyard, keeping as quiet as they could. A low voice came from the doorway where Malcolm was still hiding.

"How quick you've been! Those men have been chucking something down ever since you left. Now one of them is trying to find a way

237

down. I heard them say something about a lorry."

"Ah! So they've got a lorry hidden somewhere have they?" said the policeman. "Well, I'll just go and find it and let the air out of the tyres – then they can't get away if they get the wind up and run!"

He and James went to look for the lorry. They found it easily enough, hidden under some trees outside the churchyard. The policeman lost no time in letting the air out of the two front tyres.

By this time the second policeman was there, too, and a whispered conference took place. James was so excited that he could hardly keep still. What a thing to happen! Who would have dreamed that his great-grandpa's old telescope would have found out such a robbery!

There came the sound of quiet feet and a panting whisper. It was Malcolm. "James! Where is the policeman? That man called Eddie is climbing down a drainpipe."

The two policemen at once ran back into the churchyard – and the very first thing that happened was that they bumped into Eddie! He gave a yell and slipped away, calling out to warn the others. He tore across the churchyard and over the wall.

"He's gone for the lorry," said the policemen. "Come on."

Eddie was in the lorry and starting up the engine as the two men panted up. The lorry started off with a jolt – but the man realised at once that the tyres were flat. He gave a shout and leaped out – straight into the arms of the two policemen!

"There's a car coming!" yelled James, and just then a police car glided up, closely followed by a second. Out jumped four more policemen,

their buttons gleaming in the moonlight. What an excitement!

It wasn't long before the ladder was set up again and the two men still up on the roof were ordered down. Then the police cars drove away with the three prisoners, and the two village policemen examined the sheets of lead that had been stripped off the roof of the church.

"You two boys have done pretty good work tonight," said one policeman. "Those men are the ones that have been going round the country for a long time, stealing lead from all kinds of roofs. How did you say you managed to spot them?"

"Well – I was looking through my great-grandpa's telescope," began James – and then he stopped. "Oh my goodness – what have I done with it? I brought it with me – and now I haven't got it!"

"Is this it?" said a policeman, picking up something. James gave a cry.

"Yes – and oh dear, one of those sheets of lead must have fallen on it! It's bent and broken! It won't be any use at all. Whatever will Great-grandpa say?"

The boys went back home, very excited. They decided not to wake their parents up.

They would tell them in the morning.

You should have seen the faces of James's parents – and of his great-grandfather, too – when he told them his news at breakfast. They simply couldn't believe his story!

"Bless us all!" said Great-grandpa. "What boys do nowadays! Do you mean to say it was all because of my old telescope?"

"Yes, Great-grandpa – but I say, I do hope you won't be too cross with me! You see, in all the excitement of the night a sheet of the lead fell on the spot where I had put the telescope – and it's bent and broken."

"Now, don't you worry about that," said Great-grandpa, generously. "That old telescope wasn't much good except for you two boys to use. It won't be missed!"

"It will," said James, sadly. "It was awfully useful for bird-watching, Great-grandpa. We shall miss it very much."

A knock came at the door and somebody walked in. It was the rector of the old church. He loved it very much and had been horrified to hear how the lead from the roof had nearly been stolen. He looked at James.

"Ah, James!" he said. "I've heard about you and Malcolm from the police this morning. Where is Malcolm?"

"There he is – just coming in," said James. "Hi, Malcolm – how are you after last night?"

Malcolm came in, solemn as usual, but with a very pleased look about him, all the same. "My parents are awfully pleased," he said. "They seem quite proud of me! Good morning, everybody. Have you told your great-grandfather about the broken telescope, James?"

"Of course," said James. "Here's the rector, Malcolm. He's heard about everything, too."

"Yes," said the rector, beaming. "I came to thank you both for what you've done. And I wanted to say that I want to give you something as a little memento of such an exciting evening. Is there anything you would like, the two of you?"

"Oh, yes, sir – a pair of real binoculars," said James at once. "We'd like those better than anything!"

His mother laughed. "Oh no, James," she said. "You mustn't ask for those – they are very expensive."

"Oh," said James, and went red in the face. "I didn't know they were so expensive. Sorry, sir!"

The rector smiled all over his face. "Well, as it happens, you can have what you want," he said. "I've got an old pair – a good pair – which I never use. I'd be delighted to give them to you and Malcolm for bird-watching. I used to do it when I was a boy, but I don't have time now."

James and Malcolm share the glasses between them, and take the very greatest care of them. They have watched so many birds and animals and discovered so many things that they are keeping a diary about them. Great-grandpa is going to be allowed to read it first because, as he says, there wouldn't be any book if it hadn't been for him and his old telescope!

The Case of the Five Dogs

One day, when John was sitting reading in his garden, he heard his name called. He looked up and saw the face of a little girl peeping over the wall. "Hello, Meg, what do you want?" he asked.

"Oh, John – can we come in for a minute? There's Colin here and George, and me and Katie. We want to talk to you."

"Come on over the wall then," said John, surprised. They all clambered over. Meg and Katie were ten, George and Colin were about twelve. With them were their dogs.

"What's up?" asked John. "I say, keep your dogs in order, won't you, Dad's just planted out some new things in the beds."

The boys and girls settled down on the grass, each holding the collar of their own dog. "You see, John, we know you're an awfully good detective," said George. "So we thought you might help us. Something awful has happened."

245

"What?" asked John, feeling rather important at being called an awfully good detective.

"This morning some of Farmer Warner's sheep were chased by dogs," said George. "One fell in the stream and broke its leg."

"And the farmer went to the police and he said it was our dogs that did it," said Katie, almost in tears. "He said one of his sheep was

killed the other day by dogs, and he saw an Aberdeen like my Jock, a terrier like George's Sandy, a Sealyham like Meg's and a spaniel like Colin's in the road outside the field. So now he says it was our dogs that killed his sheep last week, and ours that chased them today."

"And perhaps they'll be shot," said Colin, gloomily. "Or else our fathers will be fined. But we know it wasn't our dogs."

"We want you to help us," said George. "You've got to prove that it was somebody else's dogs, not ours, see? You're a clever enough detective for that, aren't you?"

"Well – I don't know," said John. "This isn't quite like any case I've had before. To begin with, some dog must have killed that sheep. If we could prove that first, we'd be halfway to saving your dogs. But we don't know whose dog did it."

"Yes, we do," said Colin at once. "It was the log-man's dog – you know, the man who comes all round the district selling logs. He's got a horrible black dog, big and fierce and ugly."

"Oh, yes, I know it," said John. "It's the only dog I'm really scared of. It looks so fierce and it growls like anything if anyone goes near it. I always think it looks as bad-tempered as its master."

"Yes, that's the one," said Meg.

"But how do you know it's the dog that killed the sheep?" asked John. "Did you see it?"

"No, but we know someone who did," said George. "You know, there's a gypsy caravan near that field, and there are some children living there. One's called Julie, and we sometimes speak to her. She told us she saw the big black dog chase the sheep and kill it."

"Well, then – that's easy! She's only got to tell the police that!" said John.

"She won't. She's afraid of the police. She says if we try to make her tell, she'll say she doesn't know anything," said Colin. "She says her father would beat her black and blue if she told anything to the police. They are so scared of policemen."

"I told the policeman who came about my dog that I knew it was the big black one belonging to the log-man," said George. "But when he came again he said the log-man said he wasn't in the district that evening, so it couldn't have been his dog, because it never leaves him."

"And now it's our dogs that are getting the

blame for everything!" said Meg, fiercely, putting her arms round her Sealyham. "Why, Scamp doesn't even chase cats! I'm not going to have him shot for something that isn't his fault."

"So you see, John, you *must* do something," said Katie. "We could only think of coming to you. Will you help us?"

"Yes, of course," said John, who was very fond of dogs. "But it's going to be difficult to make a man own up to his dog killing a sheep, if he's already said that neither he nor his dog were here that evening. Have you asked if anyone else saw him or his dog that evening near Farmer Warner's sheep field?"

"Yes, we've asked everyone," said Colin. "But nobody did. You know, there was a big meeting on the green that night, and simply everyone was there. There might not have been a single person anywhere near the field when the sheep was killed – except Julie, and she won't tell."

"She ought to tell," said Meg. "That dog once snapped at their baby."

"It's an awful dog," said George. "It'll end up killing somebody. John, can you do something?"

"Well, I'll try," said John. "But somehow I

just don't know how to begin. First – what day was the sheep killed?"

"Last Friday," said Colin. "I was on the green with the others. We were listening to the speaker, and I was watching an aeroplane doing stunts in the sky. It wrote 'Moon' against the blue, and we all laughed, because it was Mr Moon who was speaking at the meeting. It was a good advertisement for him. He wants everyone to vote for him, doesn't he?"

"Fancy hiring an aeroplane to write your name in the sky!" said Meg. "I wish one would write mine. I'd feel very important."

"Well, let's get back to our subject," said John. "The sheep was killed on Friday. Julie says she saw the log-man's black dog kill it. The log-man says he wasn't here and neither was his dog. Where does he say he was, I wonder?"

"He swears he was fifteen miles away," said Colin. "Out on his bicycle, he says. He'd sold all his logs that day, and went to speak to a man at Five-Mile Hill about timber, but he wasn't there. Anyway, the log-man swears he was miles and miles away from here. He says his dog loped along beside his bike all the way. So there you are!"

"Did Julie see the log-man as well as his

black dog on Friday, when the dog killed the sheep?" said John.

"No. But she said she heard his peculiar whistle, when he whistled to the dog to come to him," said Colin. "You know his whistle? It's awfully loud and shrill. He puts two fingers in his mouth when he does it. Julie can do it too. But I can't."

"Well – it looks as if the dog and the man were there on Friday then, when everyone else was on the green listening to Mr Moon," said John. "But how in the world can we prove it?"

"The log-man is coming again tomorrow," said Meg, suddenly. "It's his day for our village. Couldn't you talk to him, John?"

"Well . . ." said John, and stopped. He didn't like the log-man, and he didn't think the log-man would like him, either. And he certainly didn't like the log-man's dog. It gave him a horrid feeling when the big black creature sniffed round his ankles. He felt as if at any moment it might take a bite out of his leg.

"Oh, please, please do," said Meg. "We'll come and be with you, if you like. But we'd better leave our dogs at home, or that awful black dog will gobble them up!"

"Yes, for goodness sake don't bring your

dogs," said John, picturing a free fight between them and the black dog going on all round him. "All right. I'll think of something to say to him. You can all be with me and listen to what he says."

The log-man always went to the village inn, when he was near, and brought out a drink for himself. He sat down on the log bench beside the green in the evening sunshine, and ate bread and cheese and drank his beer. His dog always lay at his feet.

"He'll be there about six o'clock," said John. "I often see him there then. We'll be playing about, and I'll go up and try to get him into a conversation. You can all listen hard. But don't mention the word 'dogs' or he'll be on his guard."

"Right," said Colin. "He doesn't know any of us. Now mind, everybody – leave your dogs at home so that they can't get out."

John was a bit worried about this new problem. It wasn't like his others at all. He didn't see how to tackle it, no matter how hard he puzzled about it. He lay in bed that night and pondered over it.

Julie had seen the dog killing the sheep and had heard the log-man whistling to him that Friday evening. Therefore he must have been there. But he said he was miles and miles away. Everyone else, unfortunately, seemed to have been on the green, listening to Mr Moon, and looking at his name being written in the sky. It was fortunate for the log-man that nobody was anywhere near Farmer Warner's field that evening!

After a long while John made a plan. He didn't think it was very good – but it just might work. He'd see.

So, the next evening, about six o'clock, he, Meg, Katie, Colin and George went to the green, near the Rose and Crown Inn. They began to play a game with a bat and ball. No dog was near. All had been left safely at home!

"Here's the log-man now," said John, in a low voice. "See, there's his cart. He's driving his old brown horse, and that awful black dog is sitting up beside him just as he always does."

The cart drew up outside the inn. The man got down and went inside. He came out with a tankard of beer and went to sit in the evening sunshine on a wooden bench beside the green. He pulled a packet of sandwiches out of his pocket.

"We'll give him a minute or two, then I'll go up and ask if he knows the time," said John, and threw the ball to Colin. All the children

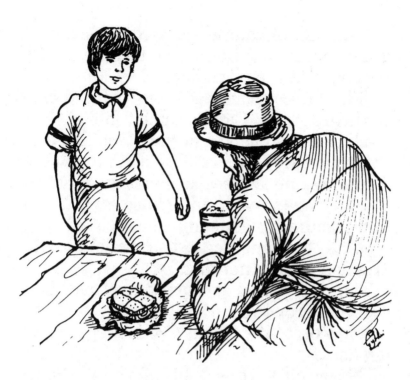

kept an eye on the black dog. He lay beside his master, but they felt that at any moment he might go after their ball.

In a little while John went up to the log-man, followed by the others. "Could you please tell me the time?" he asked.

"Look at the church clock," said the log-man, in a grumpy voice. Blow! John had forgotten that the church clock could be seen from the green.

"Oh, yes, of course – thanks," he said. "A quarter past six," he said to the others. Then he looked at the black dog.

"Fine big dog you've got," he said, politely. "I bet he eats a lot. Can he catch rabbits?"

The log-man looked at him. "My dog don't chase nothing," he said. "He don't chase even a sparrow. He just keeps alongside of me."

"But surely he would chase a cat?" said Colin, joining in. "All dogs chase cats."

"Well, this one don't," said the log-man. "He don't chase nothing."

The dog looked at them out of bloodshot eyes and growled.

"He won't bite, will he?" said Meg, retreating hastily.

"Never bit anyone in his life," said the log-man. "Best-tempered dog I ever had."

The dog growled again and showed yellow teeth. None of the children liked him at all.

"Is he afraid of anything?" asked John. "You know – afraid of guns or noises or anything like that? Some dogs are."

"No. He ain't afraid of nothing," said the log-man.

"I knew a dog once that was scared stiff of aeroplanes," said John.

"Mine don't mind nothing at all," said the

log-man and took a long drink.

"I think I can hear an aeroplane now," said John. "Oh no – it's a car. I say – have you heard of those aeroplanes that can write in the sky? I wish I could see one!"

"You did see one – don't you remember? It wrote 'moon' in the sky," said Colin, astonished at John's forgetfulness.

"No – surely it wrote 'sun'," said John. "Wait a bit – yes – I'm remembering – it wrote 'sun', didn't it?"

"Gah – it wrote 'moon', of course," said the log-man, munching hard. "Can't you read, then? It wrote 'moon' plain as anything. That's a wonderful thing that is, to write in smoke in the sky."

"Let's see – it was a white aeroplane, wasn't it?" said John, as if he was trying hard to remember. But everyone put him right.

"No, it was one of those silvery-grey ones, it was, really!"

John appealed to the log-man. "It wasn't, was it? It was white."

"You're wrong," said the log-man, and took another sandwich. "It was grey. Saw it as clear as could be. And the markings too – LGO they were, whatever they might mean. My eyes are as good as yourn any day."

257

He got up, emptied the dregs from his tankard on to the grass and went into the inn. He came out again, followed by his dog, and climbed up on to his cart. Without so much as a wave he drove off.

The children crowded round John. Only Colin had seen how his little plan had worked. The others hadn't.

"John – how very, very clever of you – to lead the conversation round to aeroplanes like that – and to make him say he'd seen that one writing 'moon' in the sky, and to make him describe it too!"

"Well – but what's so clever about all that?" said Meg.

"Can't you see, silly? That plane came over on Friday evening, and only Friday evening – and the log-man said he was miles away! Well, how could he have seen that aeroplane writing in the sky, if he wasn't here?"

There was a silence. John and Colin looked round triumphantly. "There you are!" said John. "He's admitted he was here and we've got five witnesses. Come on, we'll go to the police station."

And off they all went. John's friend the sergeant was there, and he took them into his room, looking amused. He listened to their

whole story without interrupting once. Then he made a few notes.

"Very interesting," he said, "this is very, very interesting. And very smart work too, Detective John. We will follow this up and ask the log-man how he managed to see this aeroplane doing its tricks when he was fifteen miles away."

The children next went to Julie. They told her what had happened. "Suppose the logman admits he and his dog were here, will you say what you saw?" asked Colin. "You must, you know – because you'll be a proper witness then."

Julie looked scared. "Will I get into trouble if I don't say?" she asked.

"Yes, awful trouble!" said John, hardheadedly. "Oh, Julie – surely you will speak up for our dogs – you wouldn't want them to be destroyed, would you, instead of a wicked dog that has killed a sheep and already scared your baby?"

"Well, all right then," said Julie. So when a policeman called, Julie told him all she had

seen, and, armed with this, and the other information the children had given him, the sergeant went off to interview the log-man.

He came back again in his car, and saw the children gathered together on the green, waiting for him. This time they had their dogs with them.

He stopped his car. The children crowded round him.

"Well, he's confessed," said the sergeant. "He was in the district, his dog was with him, it did go for the sheep, and then he whistled it off. He says he didn't know a sheep was killed at the time, and was too afraid to confess when he did hear. I don't know about that. Anyway, what do you think that dog did?"

"What?" asked the children. The sergeant showed them a bandaged leg.

"Tried to take a nip out of me!" he said. "Silly thing to do, wasn't it? He's going to be punished for all his misdeeds, you may be sure – and your dogs can now go home without a stain on their character – thanks to good old Detective John!"

"Woof," said the dogs at once. "Woof!" And they tried to lick John as if they did honestly understand what he had done for them. He really is a very good detective, isn't he?

261

The Wild West
Kids

Peter banged on Jill's door early one summer morning. "Jill! Get up, and let's get the horses. It's a beautiful morning, really super."

Jill sat up with a jump. She looked out of the window. The sun was streaming over the fields out of a sky as blue as forget-me-nots. Hurrah!

"All right, I'm coming," said Jill and leaped out of bed. "I'll just throw on some riding-clothes."

In a few minutes she was down in the stables with Peter. Each of them had a horse of their own, given to them by their grandfather, who was a farmer, and bred cattle, sheep and horses.

"Dear old Bunter," said Peter to the lovely chestnut horse that stamped with delight at seeing him so early in the morning. Jill's horse went to her too, nuzzling his great head against her shoulder in the way she loved.

She had called her horse Nuzzler, because of this endearing habit of his. She rubbed her hand up and down his velvety nose. "Hello, Nuzzler! Are you pleased to see me so early? What about a gallop?"

Nuzzler whinnied softly, and capered round a little, his brown eyes gleaming. That was what he loved more than anything, a swift gallop over the grassy hills on a sunny morning.

Then off went both children, first cantering and then letting Bunter and Nuzzler gallop. Peter reined in Bunter a little and then called back to Jill.

"Shall we go to our circus ring this morning? We've got plenty of time. I bet Nuzzler and Bunter would enjoy it."

"Oh yes," called back Jill. "I feel as if I could do all sorts of marvellous things on a day like this."

They galloped to a little round clearing, roughly about the size of a circus ring. Both children had ridden horses since they were two years old and they were as much at home on a horse's back as on their own feet. They had found this little "circus ring" as they called it, three or four years before, and had practised quite a number of daring tricks there.

Peter stripped off Bunter's saddle. "I'm going to do some bareback riding," he said.

"Cowboys and Indians! Hooo, Bunter! Round we go, top speed!"

Bunter knew this trick. Round and round the little green ring he went, just as if he was in a circus. He didn't mind Peter's wild Indian yells in the least. He enjoyed them. He even threw back his own head and gave a loud and exultant neigh, as if he too were whooping like an Indian!

Peter stood up on Bunter's back, and stayed there while Bunter went round and round.

He kept his balance marvellously and Jill clapped him loudly. Then down he flopped, on to Bunter's back – but rode back to front!

"Jolly good, jolly good!" yelled Jill. "Now here I come too."

She galloped into the little green ring and Nuzzler began to go round and round behind Bunter. Jill was almost as clever as Peter in the way she could stand up on Nuzzler's back. But she could not ride backwards. She always slipped off with a bump when she tried.

As the two children were performing to their heart's content, letting out wild yells at intervals, two boys came up. They also were on horses – and with them was a string of shining, satiny horses, tossing their beautiful heads and champing at their bits.

Peter and Jill did not see them at first. Then suddenly the two boys cantered into the little green ring on their own horses and joined the private circus! Round and round went the four horses, and Peter and Jill stared in sudden surprise at the newcomers.

"Go on, go on," yelled one of the boys to Peter, seeing that he was about to rein his horse to a stop. "Now, when I shout – turn your horses the other way and make them canter in the opposite direction."

He gave a loud shout: "HUP then!" His own horse and his friend's at once stopped, wheeled their heads round, and tried to go the opposite way. But, of course, Bunter and Nuzzler, not being used to this sudden change, did not turn properly – and all four horses bumped violently into one another. Jill gave a shriek and fell off. Then all four of the children collapsed into laughter.

"I say! Who are you?" asked Peter, looking with admiration at the string of horses standing patiently nearby.

"We're from the circus camp," said the bigger boy. "It's arrived this morning, down in Bolter's field over there. We're in charge of the horses. I'm Sam and he's my cousin Dan. Sam and Dan, the world's wonder-riders, the real Wild West Kids."

"Gracious!" said Jill, getting up from the ground. "Is that what you're called? Are these horses circus horses? Do you ride in the ring?"

"You bet we do," said Sam. "We've got proper Indian clothes and headdresses – and you should hear us yell."

"Aren't you lucky to belong to a circus," said Jill, enviously. "Fancy having all those glorious horses to look after, too. No wonder you ride so well if you perform in the ring."

"Well, you two kids ride pretty well too," said Dan. "We watched you. Say, your brother's as good as any circus fellow, the way he stands up to ride that horse of his. Has he rubbed any resin into its back so that he doesn't slip? We always do."

"No. Never heard of it," said Peter, feeling very pleased at this unexpected praise from a real circus-rider. "We only just mess about, you know."

"Like to come and see round the circus camp sometime?" asked Sam. "And can't you come and see us do our act some night? We're hot stuff, Dan and me."

"We'd love to," said Jill. "We'd better get back to breakfast now, though. Can we come after that?"

"Right. We'll expect you," said Sam. "Come on your horses, of course. They'll enjoy having a gossip with ours."

Jill and Peter galloped back home, thrilled. "Fantastic!" said Jill. "I've always wanted to see round a circus camp. I wonder if they've got elephants this year."

After breakfast the two galloped off to Bolter's field. It had been quiet and empty the day before but now it was crowded and full of life. Brightly painted caravans stood all about, tents had sprung up, and men were busy putting up the big top in which the circus itself was to perform that night. It was a most enormous tent.

"Two elephants!" said Jill, in delight. "And look at all those dogs. I've never seen so many

tails wagging in my life, not even at a meeting of hounds! What's in that travelling cage, I wonder? Oh, Peter, isn't this fun? I wonder where Sam and Dan are. Let's look for them."

Sam and Dan were on the look out for them. They came over to the children and grinned. "Hello! So you've come. Leave your horses here with ours and we'll show you around a bit."

The circus camp was a thrilling place to wander round. They saw the two enormous elephants, Miss Muffet and Polly Flinders. Polly played a trick on Jill. She suddenly wound her trunk round her waist, lifted her up and set her gently on her head. Jill, half frightened, gave a squeal.

"Hey, Polly! Where are your manners?" called a little man nearby. He walked up, grinning all over his comical freckled face. "Sorry, Miss, if she scared you. But she only does that to people she really likes. She must have taken a fancy to you!"

He held out his arms and somehow Jill slithered down. She felt proud that Polly had liked her so much, but she thought she would keep away from both elephants, just in case they suddenly liked her very much again!

"You must come and see them in the ring

some night," said the little elephant man. "They're grand. They play cricket with me."

Someone came swiftly up to them, turning cartwheels in a most graceful and amusing way. Immediately Sam and Dan joined in, and over and over went the three on hands and feet, like living wheels.

"Oh, teach us to do that!" begged Jill, when all three stood upright again, laughing and breathless.

"That's Tickles, the chief clown," said Dan. He didn't look like a clown at all. He looked like a rather dirty and untidy young man, with a terrific shock of hair, a very snub nose, and the widest grin the children had ever seen. He was dressed in a pullover and old flannel trousers.

"Pleased to meet you," said Tickles. He jumped into the air, turned a double somersault, landed neatly on his feet, and then turned himself upside down and walked about on his hands.

"Full of beans this morning, isn't he?" said Dan. "He's a scream in the ring. Specially when he tries to ride a horse. We've got one called Toothy, who will try to pick Tickles up whenever he falls off. They bring the house down between them."

271

"It does sound exciting," said Peter. "I wish I could walk on my hands like Tickles does."

"Well, we'll teach you if you like," said Tickles, and walked off with the little company to see an excited crowd of dogs, who were gathering round a small woman.

"That's Madame Lilliput and her performing dogs," said Dan. "See that little white one? He's a marvel. They all play football in the ring, and Tippy's goal. You should see him bump the ball away from goal with his nose."

The dogs looked very lively and well-fed and happy. They jumped up at Madame Lilliput, trying their best to lick her hands. It was plain that every dog adored her.

Taking a big football in her hands, Madame Lilliput wandered off towards the big top.

"She's going to put in some practice in the ring," said Dan. "She doesn't like being watched, or I'd take you to see those clever dogs of hers."

They wandered round the camp, looking at the caravans. They peeped inside one or two, marvelling at the amount of stuff that was packed there. All of them looked cosy and comfortable, but one or two were rather dirty and untidy.

"Who lives in that grand motor-caravan?" asked Jill, seeing a big one by itself, painted a lovely blue.

"Oh, that belongs to Jo Martini. He owns the circus," said Dan. "He's a fine fellow, but, oh! what a temper! You'll see him in the ring when you come, with his outsize whip. You'll hear him cracking it, too. It makes a simply terrific noise."

"Do you remember when we had that bad fellow here – Jeremy Hiyo – and . . . "

"Oh, yes," finished Dan, "and Jo flew into a temper with him and chased him all round the camp, cracking his great whip so cleverly that the end of it flicked Jeremy each time. Didn't he yell!"

"I've felt the end of that whip myself," said Sam. "Makes you yell all right! Look out – there's Jo himself."

A great big man came out of the blue caravan. He wore spotless white riding-breeches and a top hat. In his hand he carried the biggest whip that Jill and Peter had ever seen. He cracked it, and it went off like a pistol shot. The children jumped. Jo grinned at them.

"Good morning. Visitors, I see. Want to join my circus?"

"Oh! I wish we could!" said Jill, fervently. "But I don't expect we'd be allowed to."

"I don't expect so either," said Jo. "You have to be born to circus life if you're to be any good, you know. Trained to it from a day old. See this whip? You wouldn't believe how often I've used it on these two bad lads here."

Sam and Dan laughed. Mr Martini cracked his whip again and strode off. "Isn't he grand?" said Jill. "I feel half scared of him, but I like him all the same."

"That's what all the circus folk feel about Jo Martini," said Sam. "He's a proper ringmaster, he is – strict and stern, not afraid of using his fists and his whip, too, if anyone needs them – but kind as your own mother at home."

Peter and Jill spent the whole morning in

the camp, seeing every animal and person there. The circus folk were friendly and kindly, and the animals all seemed to be treated as if they were humans. There was a big bear there that belonged to one of the clowns, and he was so tame that he was allowed to wander about on a leash. There were monkeys, too, that leaped and chattered on the roofs of the caravans, pointing at Jill and Peter with little hairy fingers.

"They're surprised to see you," explained Dan. "They love anything strange or new. Look out for Scamp – the one over there wearing a little red hat. He's a real bit of mischief. He ran off with Jo's whip one day, and stuck it in the chimney of Tickles' caravan."

"Look – there's Madame Lilliput coming out of the big tent with her dogs," said Peter. "Has she finished practising? Can we go and see the ring?"

"Yes. And it's time we took the horses in and gave them a bit of practice there, too," said Sam. "We've got a new horse, Ladybird. She's not quite sure how to waltz yet."

Jill and Peter helped the boys to take the horses into the great ring. Sawdust was scattered in the centre. The ring was enclosed by curved pieces of wood covered with red plush. Each piece fitted against the next, and made a great red circle.

It was fun seeing the horses canter round in rhythm, nose to tail. At a shout each turned round slowly and carefully and then went the other way. Then they had to waltz. Sam started a great hurdy-gurdy going, and when the music poured out, every horse pricked up its ears.

"They love music," said Sam. "Now watch them waltz to it!"

Most of the horses managed to dance gracefully round and round, turning themselves neatly at the right moment. Jill and Peter watched in amazement. If only Bunter and Nuzzler could do that!

"See the new horse – Ladybird – she's trying her best to do what the others do," said Sam. "She's going to be a clever little thing."

"They're all beautiful," said Jill. "Absolutely beautiful. Do they wear feathery plumes at night?"

"Yes. They're as grand as can be," said Sam. "And don't they love being dressed up too! Bad as the monkeys. They just love it."

"Now you can see our Wild West act!" said Sam. The string of horses trotted docilely out

of the ring. Then in galloped Sam and Dan, whooping and yelling for all they were worth. The things they did! Jill and Peter watched in amazement.

They stood up, they sat down, they slithered right under their horses and up the other side, they stopped at top speed and reared up alarmingly, they even leaped to one another's horses and changed places.

Jill and Peter got tremendously excited and yelled loudly. Then suddenly two brown noses appeared at the tent opening, and Bunter and Nuzzler, attracted by the yells of Jill and Peter, looked in.

"Bunter! Come on! We'll join in!" yelled Peter, and Bunter trotted over to him. Nuzzler came too. In a flash both children were on their horses and in the ring as well. What a commotion there was! The four horses enjoyed it as much as the children, and soon Peter began to do things as daring as those the two boys did. When he jumped from his own horse to Sam's, Dan gave a yell.

"Look at that! Bravo, bravo!"

At last, tired out and trembling with excitement, they slowed down and trotted their horses out into the sunshine. Sam and Dan looked admiringly at Jill and Peter.

"I say! You'd be as good as we are, if you did a bit of practising."

"Do you think so?" asked Peter, eagerly. "Could we come along and practise with you sometimes? We've got holidays now. Bunter and Nuzzler would love it."

"Yes, you come," said Sam. "Then if you're ever out of a job you could always ask Jo for one in his circus!"

Jill and Peter cantered off, their eyes shining. "What a morning!" said Peter. "Gosh, we've always enjoyed messing about in our own little ring – but to practise in a real circus ring – it's marvellous!"

"It's fantastic," said Jill. "I do hope Mum won't say no."

Their mother asked a lot of questions, but she didn't say no. "You'll get tired of it after a day or two," she said. "But I've no doubt it will do you good to see how hard the circus folk have to work. You just train your horses for fun and pleasure – to the circus folk it is a way of earning a very hard living."

So morning after morning Jill and Peter rode down to Bolter's field, where the camp lay set in its circle of gay caravans. They practised hard with Sam and Dan. Nuzzler and Bunter seemed to love it. Nuzzler even managed to learn to waltz quite well, but Bunter couldn't seem to. He would turn round the wrong way and upset all the others. Sam and Dan taught the children how to turn cartwheels and somersaults. Once they lent them old Indian suits, with fringed trousers, embroidered tunics, and great feathered headdresses. Jill had never felt so grand in all her life.

"Let's make up a new Indian game," said Sam, suddenly. "You can be a squaw, Jill, belonging to Peter. We'll be enemies and capture you. We'll tie you up to a tree, and then shoot at you with arrows – then up can come Peter. We'll snatch you up, put you on our horse, and ride off. Then Peter can come thundering behind and rescue you."

Feeling a bit doubtful about all this, Jill consented. It was certainly exciting, if a bit

uncomfortable. She made a very realistic prisoner, yelling and screaming for help so loudly that Tickles the clown looked into the ring to see if she really meant it. He stayed to watch, applauding loudly.

When Peter thundered up on Bunter, and rescued Jill from Sam's horse, everyone was too excited for anything. "If only we could do that in the ring at night!" said Sam, wiping his hot face. "Wouldn't everyone love it!"

"Oh dear – I was half afraid I was going to fall off your horse, Sam, before Peter rescued me," said Jill, sitting down on the red plush ring. "Goodness, I'm hot. Oh, Nuzzler darling, don't breathe so heavily down my neck. Look, Sam, he's worried about me. He thinks it was all real, not acting!"

So he did. He hadn't been in the game, and he couldn't bear to hear Jill yelling for help. Now he was nuzzling her lovingly, trying to find out if she was all right.

"Horses are the nicest things in the world," said Jill, stroking Nuzzler's long nose.

"Madame Lilliput wouldn't agree," said Dan. "She thinks there's nothing to beat dogs."

"And the elephant man adores Miss Muffet and Polly Flinders," said Sam. "He's always saying that elephants are the cleverest animals in the world."

"And I suppose Miss Clarissa thinks her monkeys are the best," grinned Peter. "Well, give me horses and anyone else can have the rest as far as I'm concerned."

Both children had been to see the circus show two or three times. How different the circus folk looked when they were all dressed up for the ring! They were grand and beautiful. Madame Lilliput, in her short, sparkling skirt and her plume of ostrich feathers, looked like a beautiful doll, though she was the plainest little woman imaginable in real life. Tickles the clown and his friends, Spick, Span and Soapy, the other clowns, looked lively and amusing in their circus clothes – quite different from the rather dirty, untidy youths they were in daily life.

As for Mr Martini, he was really magnificent. He was dressed in gleaming white from top to toe, and even his top hat was white. His top-boots were white and so were his riding-breeches. His whip had a vivid scarlet bow, and how he cracked it! He looked wonderful as he stood in the middle of the brilliant ring, with his performers around him.

"You know, Sam, I'd give anything to go

into the ring just once," said Peter, longingly. "Just to feel what it's like – to be one of you, and one with all the animals. There can't be anything like it in the world."

"There isn't," said Sam. "It's the finest feeling there is. In the ring we're all one big family together, doing our best. We may quarrel outside in the camp, but in the ring we're the circus, we're pulling together, we're making a grand show, and aren't we proud of it!"

"I shall be awfully sorry when you go," said Jill, with a sigh. "You're all such fun. And those lovely, lovely horses. I know every single one of them now, and I don't know which I like best. Ladybird, perhaps, because she is so sweet and tries so very, very hard to do as well as the others do."

"We're giving our last show on Saturday night," said Sam. "Then we go on to our next camp. It'll be a grand show, so be sure you come. Jo says he'll give you two of the best seats that Saturday."

"Of course we'll be there," said Peter. "Mum and Dad are coming too, but they won't want to be in the front. Mum doesn't like to be too near. Heaps of the boys and girls of our school are coming too, so be sure to do your best."

"You bet!" grinned Sam. "We'll yell to you when we gallop by in our Wild West act."

"We've told everybody about you," said Jill. "Simply everybody. They'll all be looking out for you and they'll clap you like anything."

"They'll think you're marvellous," said Peter. "Gosh – I wish they could see us performing too – we're almost as good as you are now."

Saturday morning came. Peter and Jill rode down to the camp, feeling rather sad. It wouldn't be there the next day. It would be on the road, rolling away to another field. How they would miss Sam and Dan and the horses.

"Good thing that school begins again next week," said Peter. "I should feel lost without anything to do. What fun we've had!"

When they got to the camp they noticed something stra' /e. There did not seem to be anyone abou' /here could they be?

"What's happened to everyone?" said Jill, in wonder. "Oh look – there's somebody coming out of the big top."

It was Madame Lilliput coming out of the great circus tent, hurrying as fast as she could. When she saw the two children, she ran towards them, her face screwed up as if she was crying. When she came nearer, the children saw to their horror that tears were running down her cheeks.

"What's the matter? Oh, what's happened?" cried Jill, scared.

"It's Sam," said Madame Lilliput. "He climbed up to the top of the tent to put the lamp straight – and he fell. Oh, poor, poor Sam! What shall we do? We need a doctor, quickly."

Jill's heart went cold. Sam! Cheerful, lively, kindly Sam. Tears came into her eyes.

Peter sat still on his horse. Sam had fallen from the top of the tent down to the ring below! He must be very badly hurt indeed.

"Listen," he said. "Our father is a doctor. I'll ride back home and get him to come at once. He'll be here in a jiffy. Don't move Sam till he comes."

The boy flew off like the wind on Bunter. Jill heard the thud of the hoofs as he went, but she did not go with him. She wanted to see poor Sam.

She slipped off her horse and walked on trembling legs to the big circus tent with Madame Lilliput. Everyone was inside, even the dogs and the monkeys. In the centre of the ring lay poor Sam. His eyes were shut and he was as white as a sheet. Mr Martini was kneeling over him, almost as white as Sam himself. Tickles the clown was trying to keep everyone back.

"Don't crowd round," he said in a shaky voice, not a bit like his own. "Give the poor lad a bit of air, can't you?"

Madame Lilliput went up to Mr Martini. "Jo! There's a doctor coming. He'll be here soon. Best not move the lad at all. Peter's gone for his father, who's a doctor."

The circus folk looked immensely relieved. They had been as frightened as the children when they heard of Sam's fall, but now they cheered up a bit.

286

Jill was still very worried. She had heard her father talk many times of illnesses and accidents, and she was afraid that Sam might be seriously damaged, perhaps for life.

"Poor, poor Sam," she thought. "Suppose he can never ride again? And poor Dan too. He's so fond of Sam, and they do such wonderful things together. And there's tonight too – the last night of all, when they'd planned to put on such a fine show. What a terrible bit of bad luck!"

Peter had found his father about to set out on his calls. He turned his car round at once and set off in the direction of the circus. He knew all about Sam and Dan from his children. He was at the camp in four minutes and drove his car into the field through the gate, bumping over the ruts.

Then he was in the big tent, making his way through the anxious folk. "Turn them all out," he said to Jo. "Every one of them." And out they went. Jill and Dan were allowed to stay, with Jo – and in a little while Madame Lilliput stole back to see if she could help.

Sam opened his eyes and groaned. Peter's father examined the boy quickly and carefully. Then he stood up.

"He'll be all right, thank goodness. He's not

damaged himself too much. He'll have to go to hospital and have treatment – and he'll be very sore and bruised for a few days. There'll be no riding for him for a month or two, though."

Tears ran down Dan's face – a curious mixture of tears, really. He was crying for joy because Sam wasn't seriously injured – and for grief because now he wouldn't be able to ride with Sam for a long time. Jill sniffed too. She knelt down by Sam and stroked his hand.

"You're not too badly hurt, Sam," she said. "You'll be all right. Poor old Sam!"

Sam tried to say something and couldn't. He looked very worried indeed. He tried again.

"What is it, old son?" the doctor asked gently. "Don't worry about anything. You won't do yourself any good if you do. Things will be all right."

"It's tonight," said Sam, with an effort. "See? It's the big show tonight. What about – the Wild West Kids?"

"That's all right," said Jo. "We'll do without them."

"No," said Sam. "No. There's Dan. Don't leave him out. Jill, you and Peter – can't you do it with Dan?"

"Now don't worry yourself like this," said the doctor, anxiously. But Jill pulled at his arm.

"Daddy! Why shouldn't Peter and I help Dan tonight in the ring? We know everything! We've practised it time and time again. Even Sam says we're as good as he and Dan are!"

Peter was now back and he joined in eagerly. "Yes, Dad – we can do the Wild West act. We've got a very good one, with Jill as a squaw. You've seen it too, haven't you, Mr Martini?"

Jo nodded. He had come into the ring once while the four of them were doing it, and had been amused and surprised. He looked at Peter's father.

"They're good," he said. "And if it would

289

set Sam's mind at rest – and if you wouldn't
mind, Doctor, why I'd be pleased to give your
kids a chance in the ring. They'd love it – it
would be a reward to them for all the
practising they've done with Sam and Dan
here. But it's for you to decide."

The doctor looked down at Sam. The boy's
eyes were shining and colour had come back to
his face. He caught hold of the doctor's hand
feebly. "Give them a chance," he begged. "Let
the show go on just the same without me, but
with Dan and Peter and Jill. I'll feel happy
then."

"All right," said the doctor, and Peter and Jill
looked at one another with shining eyes. Poor
Sam – it was because of him they had their
chance, and they were immensely sorry for
him – but they could not help feeling excited
and happy to think of the coming night.

"We'll do our best, Sam," said Jill, and the
boy nodded, looking happy.

"Help me to lift him gently to my car," said
the doctor to Jo. "I'll take him to hospital
myself. You can come with us, Dan. Not you,
Jill and Peter. That would be too big a crowd
for Sam. I'll look after the boy, Mr Martini, till
he's better, and keep you posted about him."

"Thanks, Doctor," said Jo, gratefully. "He's

got no father or mother. There's only me and I'm his guardian. He's a good lad. Aren't you, Sam?"

Sam tried to put on a grin. He was in pain and it was difficult, but he managed a faint one. Then he was carried gently to the car and laid comfortably on the back seat.

That evening the three, Dan, Jill and Peter, were in a state of the greatest excitement. Dan, wild and lively after the shock and grief of the morning, shouted and laughed. Peter and Jill dressed themselves in their Indian clothes, and Jill found that her hands were

shaking with excitement. She could hardly do up her tunic.

All the circus folk came to wish them luck. "It's grand of you to step in like this, so that Dan can carry on," said Tickles. "Our last show in a place is always the best. You'll be fine!"

"I hope so," said Peter, feeling suddenly nervous. "You know, Tickles, all our school friends will be there. Can't think what they'll say! And Mum and Dad are coming too. I hope we shan't do anything silly."

"You'll be all right," said Tickles. "We shall all be fine tonight. We're all feeling glad that Sam isn't hurt too badly. He'll be back with us again before the winter, as good as ever, your father says. Say, he's a grand fellow, your father, isn't he? If I wasn't a clown, I'd be a doctor. Next best thing to making people laugh would be to make them well when they're ill. I wouldn't mind being a doctor at all."

Peter smiled. Funny old Tickles. Then he began to worry about his part in the show again. Would he really be able to do it all right? Would Bunter be nervous?

Neither Bunter nor Nuzzler were nervous. They were excited and happy. Somehow they sensed that for once they were one with all the other horses. They were The Circus. Bunter whinnied a little and Nuzzler nuzzled against him.

The grand parade began to the lively strains of the band. Into the ring went every performer, both human and animal, parading round in their finery, lifting their hands to

greet the clapping audience. And into the ring went Jill and Peter too on Bunter and Nuzzler, following Dan. The children were all dressed in their Indian costumes, ready for their act later on. Their hearts were beating fast. They waved their hands too, and tried to see the faces of their parents in the vast audience.

"Hey, there's the Wild West Kids!" shouted a shrill voice. Peter knew that voice. It belonged to Bobby, a boy in his form. "Hey, look! There's three of them, not two, tonight."

Peter waved his hand to Bobby. Bobby did not recognise him in his Indian clothes, but he was thrilled that one of the Wild West Kids had actually waved to him.

"See that," he said proudly to his companions. "He waved to me. Gosh, wouldn't I like to be in his shoes tonight!"

The grand parade was over. The show began. In came the beautiful horses to canter round and round, and to waltz and do their tricks. How they enjoyed every moment. Everybody clapped wildly at the sight of the sleek, shining creatures, and Mr Martini cracked his whip and looked at them proudly. This was his great moment. He was the grand man of the circus, the ringmaster, and these beautiful horses were his. He wouldn't have changed places for anyone on earth at that moment.

"Good old Jo!" whispered the watching circus folk to one another.

Crack! went his whip, and the horses changed round and went in the opposite direction, while the band kept time to their cantering.

One after another the turns came on. Tickles and the clowns sent the audience into fits of laughter. They had never been so funny before. When Tickles tried to ride a horse and fell off every time, Bobby and the others from Peter's school cried with laughter. It made Jill and Peter laugh to see them.

The elephants played cricket with their trainer, and the dogs played football with Madame Lilliput. Their eager barking filled the ring, and when the little goalkeeper dog saved goal after goal the audience cheered and clapped with admiration!

"What a fine show!" said Bobby to the others. "What's next? Oh, the Wild West Kids. Good!"

And into the ring rode Dan, Jill and Peter! As soon as the time came for them to appear, all their nervousness went. Instead they were filled with a wild excitement and they galloped

in, whooping and yelling as if they really were Indians!

The children in the audience clapped and stamped vigorously. This was what they liked. They shouted and yelled as much as the Indians did, when they saw the tricks they performed.

Round the ring they went at top speed. Then up on the horses' backs they all stood. Then down they sat, facing their horses' tails. Yes, even Jill could manage that now without sliding off. Then up they stood again, and Peter and Dan changed horses by jumping from one to the other.

"Good gracious!" said Peter's mother to his father. "I didn't know they could do this kind of thing! Is it safe? Oh my goodness, there they go again. Well, I never thought Peter and Jill would go careering round a circus ring, performing like that!"

Then the three did their act where Jill was the squaw. Dan rode off with her and then tied her up to a post. He shot arrows at her, missing her cleverly, and she screamed so realistically that her mother almost went into the ring to rescue her herself!

Then up thundered Peter, whooping for all he was worth. How the audience cheered him!

Dan snatched at Jill, got her on his horse, and galloped off with her round the ring. After him went Peter, whirling a lasso, which was another trick he had learned. He neatly lassoed Dan and drew him to a standstill.

Then he snatched Jill off Dan's horse, put her on his, and rode off with her at top speed while Bobby and the rest cheered frantically at the tops of their voices.

Dan rode out of the ring after Peter. But in a second they were back again with Jill to take their bows. They leaped off their horses and bowed time and again. Then they did a series of cartwheels round their horses, leaped to their feet and vaulted on to their horses' backs. Off they went out of the ring to a perfect tornado of applause.

Peter's parents clapped madly too. They could not believe that Jill and Peter were so good. As for the circus folk they crowded round them and slapped them on the back till they were sore. Mr Martini strode up and held out his great hairy hand.

"Fine, fine! Bravo! Best act I've seen any kids do for years! If ever you want a job, you two, come along to me and I'll give you one in my circus. See! If your father and mother ever turn you out of house and home, you'll know where to come to!"

"Thanks, sir," said Peter, glowing, "but I don't think that's likely to happen somehow. All the same – it's a great feeling to go into the ring and I'll never, never forget it!"

They stayed behind to have supper with the circus folk, and their mother and father came too. After supper the camp was to start on its journey to its next camping place. It was to travel in the quiet of the night. The moon was bright, the roads were empty. In an hour's time the caravans would be on their way, and the lorries would follow after, packed with all the circus properties.

"So it's goodbye," said Mr Martini at the end of the hilarious meal. He held out his hand. "Pleased and proud to have met you. Good as any circus kids you are, and that's saying a lot. Goodbye. Look after Sam for me and send him back as soon as he's fit."

All the goodbyes were said. Jill and Peter could not help feeling a little sad as they shook hands with Tickles, the elephant man, Madame Lilliput and the rest. They patted all the horses, shook paws with the monkeys and with the performing dogs too.

"We'll come back next year," said Mr Martini, getting into his blue caravan. "See you then. And maybe you can do a Wild West act again, with Sam and Dan, if your parents will let you. Goodbye."

The line of caravans crawled out of the field gate and on to the road. The moon shone down

on the little houses on wheels. Dogs barked and the two elephants, who were walking, trumpeted loudly.

"They're saying goodbye too," said Jill. "Oh Peter, do you think Bobby and the rest will believe it was us, when we tell them next week at school?"

"We'll see," said Peter with a grin. "Old Sam will be thrilled when he hears about it, won't he?"

The next week Peter spoke to Bobby and the others at his school. "Did you see the circus on Saturday? Did you like it?"

"Oh boy! Did we like it? It was super, fantastic, tremendous!" said Bobby, beaming. "Why, weren't you there? Come to think of it, I didn't see you."

"Yes. We were there," said Peter, grinning. "You saw us all right."

"I didn't," said Bobby. "I looked all round for you. You ought to have gone, you really ought."

"What did you like the best?" asked Peter. And, of course, he got the answer he hoped for.

"The best? Why, the Wild West Kids of course!" cried Bobby, and the others yelled in agreement. "You ought to have seen them, Peter – they were amazing. I'd have loved to be them, wouldn't you?"

"Yes, I would," said Peter, grinning still more widely. "And what's more, I was one of them. What do you think of that, Bobby!" And he gave such a wild Indian yell that everyone jumped. Then he did six cartwheels round the classroom, and ended up by colliding with the headmaster who was just coming in at the door.

"Now, my boy! Do you imagine that you are a circus performer?" asked the headmaster, sarcastically.

And Peter answered at once. "Well, yes, sir – I do!"

A Night
on Thunder Rock

"Dad, we've got something to ask you," said Robert. "We do hope you'll say yes."

"Well, I'm not promising till I know what it is," said his father, cautiously. "I've been caught that way before!"

"It's something quite simple," said Rita.

"Yes, something you'd love to do yourself," said Phil. "It's this – can we spend a night on Thunder Rock?"

Thunder Rock was a tiny rocky island not far out from the coast. The three children had a small boat of their own, and were used to rowing about by themselves. They had often rowed to Thunder Rock and had a picnic there.

"So now you want to spend a night there," said their father. "Well, what does your mother say?"

"She says we must ask you," said Robert. "Say yes, Dad. Only just one night. It would be such fun to camp out there all by ourselves."

"We'd take rugs and things," said Rita.

"We'd choose a very fine warm night. It would be heavenly to go off to sleep at night with the waves beating on the rocks round us, and the stars twinkling above us."

"And waking up in the morning with the sun, and slipping into the water first thing for a swim," said Phil. "Come on, Dad – say yes."

"Well, what about that old boat of yours?" said his father. "I heard it was leaking. Is it safe?"

"Pretty safe, because we can always bale out the water," said Rita. "We don't mind. Anyway, we can all swim and we'll wear our life-jackets. But I don't think the poor old boat will last much longer, Daddy. Are new boats very expensive?"

"Very," said her father. "No hope of getting one, so don't make plans. You'll have to make the leaky old tub do for some time – but mind, if it gets too bad we'll have to scrap it. No good running into danger, and you never know!"

"Well – can we go to Thunder Rock for the night?" asked Phil. "You haven't said yet."

His father smiled. "Okay – you can go. Take your food with you, and rugs and things. You'll be all right. It is fun to camp out on a little

306

island like that. You feel so very much all on your own."

"Oh, thanks, Dad! We never thought you'd say yes."

In delight the three children rushed off to their mother to tell her. "Well, I do hope you'll all be all right," she said. "You're old enough to look after yourselves now – Robert is fourteen and very strong. Don't get up to any silly tricks though. And be sure that old tub of yours doesn't leak too much."

The children said nothing about their boat. It really was leaking very badly, and needed a lot of baling to keep it from sinking lower and lower! But if only it would last till they had had their night on Thunder Rock.

being all by ourselves like that, too. Nobody to
send us here and there, nobody to ask what
we're up to, nobody to say we're making too
much noise."

They said goodbye and set off in the boat.
Everything had been piled in. Had they
forgotten anything? No, they didn't think so.
Robert pulled at the oars and Rita and Phil
baled hard.

"Bother this leak!" said Rita. "It's getting
worse. I honestly don't think the poor old tub
will last much longer."

"Well, Ted the fisherman says it's too old
to mend," said Robert, pulling hard. "Say
when you're tired of baling, Rita, and I'll have
a turn and you can row."

Gulls cried loudly all round them. The sea
was very calm, and only a slight swell lifted the

boat now and again. The sun shone from the western sky, and the water gleamed blue and purple and green. Lovely!

They got to Thunder Rock at last. They pulled the boat into a tiny cove, out of reach of the waves. Rita took out the rugs and old coats and spread them on a sandy place between some high rocks.

"We'll be well sheltered here," she said. "And the sand is warm and soft. Won't it be gorgeous sleeping out here? Now what about supper?"

Supper was lovely. Tinned salmon, tinned pineapple, new bread and butter, chocolate and lemonade. "Better than any meal on a table," said Phil. "Now let's have a look round Thunder Rock and then have a swim when our supper's settled a bit."

Thunder Rock was a strange little island. It was nothing but rocks and coves. Nothing grew on it at all, except seaweed. The seabirds came to it, and liked to stand on the highest rocks, gazing out to sea. They fluttered away a little when the children came near to them, but did not fly right off.

"Lovely things," said Rita, watching a big gull alight. "I wouldn't mind being a gull – swimming, flying, paddling, gliding, diving – what a nice life!"

They had their swim and then lay on their rugs in the twilight, warm and glowing. They put on pyjamas, and then Phil yawned.

"Golly, are you sleepy already?" said Rita. "I'm not. I want to enjoy every minute of this exciting evening. Don't let's go to sleep yet."

"Of course we won't," said Robert, nibbling a bar of chocolate. "The sun's quite gone now. There's not a single bit of pink cloud left in the sky. But it's still very warm."

"The waves sound nice, splashing all round Thunder Rock," said Rita, looking sleepy. They went on talking for a while, and then Phil gave another yawn, a most enormous one this time.

"I really don't believe I can keep awake," he said. "I do want to, but my eyes keep closing. I bet we'll sleep well tonight – with nothing whatever to disturb us except the sound of the sea."

"All right. We'll say goodnight then," said Rita. "I feel sleepy, too. I'm going to fix my eyes on that bright star over there and see how long I can keep awake. It's so lovely out here all alone on Thunder Rock."

It was not long before they were all asleep. The stars shone in the sky, and the sea splashed quietly on the rocks. There was no other sound to be heard.

But wait a minute – *was* there no other sound? Robert suddenly woke up with a jump. He lay there for a moment, wondering where he was. How strange to see the sky above him instead of the ceiling of his bedroom. Then he remembered – of course, he was on Thunder Rock. Good!

He was just about to go to sleep again when he heard the sound that had woken him. It was an extra loud splash – and then another and another. Regular splashes.

Robert sat up. It sounded like a boat being rowed along, not far from Thunder Rock. Then he heard low voices. That really made him pay attention. A boat near Thunder Rock – and voices in the middle of the night. What did it mean?

Cautiously Robert awoke Phil and whispered in his ear. "Don't make a sound. There's a boat being rowed to Thunder Rock. I can hear it – and voices too."

The boys sat and listened. But the boat did not come to Thunder Rock after all. It went right round it and the voices died away. The splash of the oars could no longer be heard.

"The boat's on the landward side of the rock now," whispered Robert. "Let's go round and see if we can spot it. There's only starlight to see by but we might just make it out."

They walked cautiously over the rocks and round to the other side of the little island. They could see a dark mass some way off –

that must be the boat! But who was in it –
and why come rowing over the sea at this time
of night? Where to? And where from?

"It's all jolly mysterious," said Robert. "Now
let's think. Where is that boat heading for?"

"It's going towards the rocky cliffs of the
mainland," said Phil. "I should think towards
the part that is always washed by the sea – the
part we've never been able to explore properly
because you can't get round to it."

"There might be caves there," said Robert.
"I wonder where the boat came from, though.
It seemed to come from out at sea – and yet it
was only rowed."

"Do you know – I bet that it came from a motor-launch some way out," said Phil, suddenly. "They wouldn't dare to bring it right in if they were doing anything they shouldn't because the motor would be heard. I bet the boat left the launch right out at sea – and was rowed in quietly, with something illegal on board. Probably they've come from France."

"Do you mean smuggled goods?" said Robert in sudden excitement. "My word – smugglers!"

"Well, you know there are still plenty of smugglers about," said Phil. "I bet you anything you like we've just heard a boat-load of smugglers passing, with smuggled goods in the boat, and they're heading for the cliffs, where they've either got a hiding-place or friends to take the goods from them."

Robert whistled. He gazed towards the dark land which could be faintly seen as a black blur in the starlit night. "Yes. You may be right. Smugglers! I say, what are we going to do about it?"

"Let's go and wake Rita," said Phil. "We can talk about it then, all together. Well, I feel wide awake now, don't you?"

Rita was very excited when she heard the boys' news. "You might have woken me before," she said indignantly. "Do you suppose the smugglers' boat will come back?"

"Well – yes – I suppose it might," said Robert. "I hadn't thought of that. We'd better keep a look-out."

They all went round to the other side of the little island and strained their eyes towards the distant cliffs. Then Robert gave an exclamation.

"Look – I'm sure I can see a light – it must be at the bottom of the cliffs, I should think."

They all stared hard, and soon Rita and Phil could see a faint light, too.

"I bet that's where the smugglers are, with their goods!" said Robert.

They sat and watched and talked for a long time. The light disappeared. Then suddenly Robert's sharp ears heard something and he clutched Rita and Phil, making them jump.

"They're coming back! Shh!" And then there came the sound of oars again, and a murmur of voices.

The boat passed in the darkness, a blur against the water. The children hardly dared to breathe. They began to whisper when the boat was out of hearing.

"They must have put the goods in a cave. Let's go tomorrow and find out."

"Shh! Listen! I believe I can hear a motor

starting up a good way out. I bet the smugglers are off back to France."

"I wish daylight would come. I want to go off and hunt for the smuggled goods!"

But day did not come. It was still only the middle of the night and the children fell asleep again and could hardly believe, in the morning, that anything had happened in the night.

"But it must have, because we all know about it," said Rita. "So it can't have been a dream. Let's have breakfast and then go and explore those cliffs. We can row quite near to them."

So after a meal they set off in their leaky old boat. They rowed towards the towering, rocky cliffs, round whose base the sea washed continually. They came nearer and nearer, and then, when they were afraid of going on the rocks, they rowed round the cliffs, examining every foot of them as carefully as they could.

And they found what they were looking for! They came suddenly to a cleft in the cliff, and guided their boat carefully towards it. A wave took them into the inlet and they found themselves in an enclosed channel, walled in by steep cliffs, with not much more room than the boat needed for itself.

On one side of the channel was a cave,

running into the cliff, quite hidden from the sea outside. "You hold the boat steady by hanging on to this rock, Phil, and I'll have a look in the cave," said Robert. He leaped from the boat on to a rock and then peered into the cave. He gave a yell.

"I say! Stacks of things! Crates and packing cases of all kinds. This is where those smugglers put their stuff. I bet someone on the mainland collects them when it's safe to do so – probably by boat."

He went back to the boat and got in. "I'd like to undo some of those crates," he said. "But I suppose I'd better not. It's a matter for the police now."

"Is it really?" said Rita, looking rather scared. "Well, come on then. Let's get back home."

They shoved the boat down through the cleft of the cliff and back to the open sea again. Robert and Phil took the oars. Phil gave a shout of dismay.

"I say! You'll have to bale like fury, Rita, the boat's awfully full of water. We'll be swimming soon! Get the baler, quick."

Certainly the boat was leaking worse than ever. Rita began to bale quickly. The boys rowed hard. But the boat was now heavy with water and it was difficult going. In the end the boys had to stop rowing and help Rita with the baling.

When they had got the boat a good bit lighter, they took the oars again.

"You'll have to hurry up," said Rita, anxiously. "It's already beginning to fill again. It must have sprung another leak. I hope we get back before it fills and sinks!"

The boat began to fill quickly again. The boys rowed hard. Just before they got to shore the boat quietly began to sink beneath them.

They had to get out and wade to shore,
carrying what they could of their goods.

"That's very bad luck," said Robert, sadly. "I
liked that old boat. I'm afraid it's done for
now. Come on, let's go home and tell Mum
what's happened. Then she can ring up the
police."

Their mother was amazed at all they had to
tell. She was horrified about the boat, and
very glad they had got home safely, though
they were very wet.

"I can hardly believe this tale of smugglers,"
she said. "But I suppose I'd better ring up the
police. I'll do it now, while you go and put on
dry things."

It wasn't long before a police inspector was
round in his car. He listened with the greatest

interest to all that the children told him.

"I expect they've really hit on something," he told their mother. "We know smuggling is going on all round the coast. But it's difficult to trace. I'll get a boat and go round to this cave. Perhaps I could take the children's boat and they could direct me to the place."

"It's sunk," Phil said, rather sorrowfully. "We haven't got a boat! We feel very upset about it. Ted the fisherman will lend you his. We'll come too."

The inspector found that the crates in the cave contained guns and ammunition, most certainly smuggled. "My word, this is a haul!" he said in delight. "Well, we'll remove all this tonight when nobody is likely to see us, and then we'll set a watch for the smugglers' friends, whoever they are. They are sure to come to fetch it soon. And we will also put somebody on Thunder Rock, lying in wait for the smugglers when they come again, as they are sure to do."

It all sounded very exciting indeed. The children wanted to go to Thunder Rock with the watchers, but the inspector said no. "There may be danger – shooting, for instance," he said. "You can't be involved in things like that. I'll let you know what happens, never fear!"

He kept his word, and brought them a very exciting story the next week. "We've got the men who receive the guns," he began. "We caught them rowing round to the cave to fetch them. And now we've got the smugglers too! Three of them!"

"Did you catch them in their boat?" asked Rita.

"We followed their boat when it went back to the open sea," said the inspector. "And there, sure enough, was a smart little motor-launch waiting for them. We got the whole lot – so that spot of smuggling is stopped for a little while at any rate."

"What a good thing we went to spend the night on Thunder Rock," said Phil. "It's bad luck our boat is gone, though."

"Oh, I wouldn't worry about that," the inspector said in an airy voice. "We want to give you a reward for your help – you'll find it in Ted the fisherman's charge if you care to go and look."

The children tore down to the beach and found Ted there, grinning. Beside his boat lay another one, newly-painted and smart.

"Good morning," said Ted. "Come to have a look at your new boat? Smart, isn't it? My word, you're lucky children, aren't you?"

"We are!" said Rita, in delight. "Bags I row it first! Oh, what a beauty. Come on, boys – haul it down the beach. Off we go!"

And off they went, bobbing lightly up and down on the waves. They rowed to Thunder Rock, pulled the boat up on the sand and lay down in the sun.

"Good old Thunder Rock!" said Phil, banging the sand below him with his open hand. "If it hadn't been for you we'd never have got that marvellous – wonderful – super – new boat!"

A Week Before
Christmas

The Jameson family were making their Christmas plans. They sat round the table under the lamp, four of them – Mother, Robert, Ellen and Betsy. Daddy was far away across the sea and wouldn't be home for Christmas.

"Now, we haven't got much money," said Mother, "so we must spend it carefully this Christmas. We can't afford a turkey, but I can get a nice big chicken. I've made a Christmas pudding, and I shall buy as much fruit as I can for you. Perhaps I shall make mince pies for a treat!"

"Can we afford a little Christmas tree?" asked Betsy. She was ten and loved a pretty Christmas tree hung with all kinds of shiny things. "Just a little one, Mummy, if we can't afford a big one."

"Yes, I'll see what I can do," said Mother, writing it down on her list. "And I've made the cake, a nice big one. I've only got to ice it and put Christmassy figures on it. I'll see if I can buy a little red Father Christmas to go in the middle."

She wrote down, *Little Father Christmas*, and then wrote something else down below. "What have you written?" asked Betsy, trying to see. But her mother covered up the words.

"No – I'm writing down what you three want for Christmas! It's not really a secret because you've all told me – and I shall try my hardest to get them."

Betsy wanted a big doll. She had never had a really big one, though she was ten. She knew she was getting a bit old for dolls now but she did so love them, and she longed to have a big one before she really was too old.

Robert wanted a model aeroplane kit. He had seen one in a shop and longed for it. It would be marvellous to put all the parts together, and at last have a model aeroplane that he could take to school for all the boys to see.

Ellen wanted a proper box of watercolours because she loved to paint and she was really very good at it.

"They're all rather expensive presents," said Ellen to Robert and Betsy, when they had discussed what they wanted. "We mustn't mind if Mummy can't get them. But she did

say we must tell her what we really wanted. I
know what she wants – a new handbag.
They're expensive too, but if we all put our
money together we might be able to buy her
the red one we saw the other day."

So they made their Christmas plans, and
discussed everything together. Since their
father had been away Mother had always
talked over everything with the children. They
knew she hadn't a great deal of money and
they helped her all they could.

"Tomorrow I'm going to go out and do my
Christmas shopping," Mother said. "I've got to

deliver all the parish magazines for the vicar,
too, because his sister who usually does it is ill.
I'll do that first, then I'll go and order the
chicken and the fruit and sweets – and perhaps
some crackers if they're not too expensive.
And I'll see if I can buy your presents too – so
nobody must come with me!"

"I'll help with the magazines," said Robert.
But his mother shook her head.

"No – you break up tomorrow and there
will be plenty for you to do. You're one of the
boys that has promised to go back in the
afternoon and help to clean up the school,
aren't you?"

"Yes," said Robert. His mother was proud of
him because whenever there was a job to be
done Robert always offered to help. "But I'll be
back in good time for tea, Mum."

The girls broke up the next day too. Then
there would be six days till Christmas – days to
decorate the house with holly from the woods,
to make paperchains to go round the walls,
to decorate the Christmas tree, paint
Christmas cards, and do all the jolly things
that have to be done before Christmas Day.

"Ellen, you put the kettle on for tea and lay
the table, because I shall be a bit late coming
back from my shopping this afternoon," said

Mother, the next day. "I'll try not to be too late – but those magazines take rather a long time to deliver and I must do my shopping afterwards."

"I'll have tea all ready, Mum," said Ellen. "I'll make you some toast."

Robert went off to help at his school. Ellen sat down to draw some Christmas cards. Betsy joined her. The afternoon passed very quickly.

"Do you know it's snowing very, very hard?" Ellen said suddenly. "Just look at the enormous flakes falling down, Betsy."

They got up and went to the window. The ground was already thickly covered with snow. "Good!" said Betsy. "Snow for Christmas! That always seems right somehow. And we'll have fun with snowballs and making snowmen."

"Mum won't like shopping much in this blinding snow," said Ellen. "Good thing she's got her winter boots on. Isn't it dark, too? I suppose that's the leaden sky. It looks like evening already."

The snow went on falling all the afternoon. By teatime it was very thick on the ground. Robert came in puffing and blowing, and shook the snow off his coat. "Goodness, it's snowy! If it goes on like this we'll be snowed up in the morning!"

Ellen put the kettle on for tea and began to cut some bread and butter. Betsy laid the table. Then she went to the window to look for her mother. But it was dark now and she could see nothing but big snowflakes falling by the window.

"I wish Mummy would come," she said. "She *is* late. She'll be awfully tired."

Mother was late. The kettle had been boiled two or three times before she came. She opened the front door and came in rather slowly. Betsy rushed to her to help her to take off her snowy things. Ellen made the tea.

"Poor Mum! You'll be cold and hungry," she called. Mother didn't say much. She took off her clothes, put them to dry, and then came in to tea. Robert looked at her in surprise. She was usually so cheerful and happy. He saw that she looked sad – and yes, it looked as if she had been crying too. He got up quickly and went to her.

"Mum! What's the matter? Has anything happened?"

"Yes," said Mother, and sat down in her chair. "I've lost my purse with all my Christmas money in! Oh children, I've looked and looked for it everywhere, and I can't find it. I must have dropped it when I was taking

the big bundle of magazines round."

The children stared at her in dismay. "Oh, Mummy! All your money in it? Don't worry, we'll help you look for it."

They all put their arms round her. She tried to smile at them but their kindness made tears come suddenly into her eyes. She blinked them away.

"It's my own stupid fault. I should have been more careful. I can't think how it happened – and now this thick snow has come and hidden everything. I'll never find it!"

The children looked at one another in despair. If the Christmas money was gone, it meant no chicken – no sweets – no fruit – no presents! Not even a Christmas tree!

"You drink a hot cup of tea, Mum, and you'll feel better," said Ellen. "We'll manage somehow."

"We've got the cake and the pudding anyhow," said Betsy. "But, oh dear," she said secretly to herself, "I shan't have that doll now – and next year I'll be too old to ask for one." But she didn't say a word of this out loud, of course. She was much too unselfish for that.

"I'll go out and look for your purse tomorrow morning," said Robert.

"The snow will be so thick by then that you wouldn't be able to see anything – even if you knew where to look!" said his mother. "I don't mind for myself, children – but it's dreadful to think you three won't be able to have anything nice for Christmas – not even the lovely presents I had planned to give you."

"Don't bother about that," said Robert. "*We*

shan't mind. Come on – let's have tea and forget about it."

But, of course, they couldn't really forget about it. They pretended to talk cheerfully but inside they all felt miserable. When Mother went in to see Mrs Peters next door, they began to talk about it.

"We shall have to do something about this," said Ellen. "Mum will be awfully unhappy if she can't even buy a chicken for Christmas Day. We must make plans."

"What plans?" asked Betsy.

"Well – to earn a bit of money ourselves. Even if it's only enough to buy a chicken or a few tangerines, it will be something," said Ellen.

There was a pause. Then Robert spoke suddenly and firmly. "I know what I'm going to do. The butcher's boy is ill and can't deliver all the Christmas orders. If I offer to deliver them the butcher would pay me a wage. That will be my bit of help."

"Oh – what a very good idea!" said Betsy. "I wish I could be an errand-girl."

"You're too small," said Robert. "You can't do anything. Ellen, can you think of anything you can do?"

"Yes, I think so," said Ellen. "You know Mrs

Harris? Well, she wants somebody to take her three little children for walks each afternoon. I could do that. They're nice little children."

"Oh, good," said Robert. "Yes, that would bring in a bit of money too. It's a pity Betsy is too young to do anything."

Betsy felt sad. She didn't like being the only one who couldn't earn anything for Christmas. She wondered and wondered what she could do. She even lay awake in bed that night, wondering. And then, just before she fell asleep, she thought of something.

She remembered a blind lady who lived in the next street. What was her name? Yes, Mrs Sullivan. Mrs Sullivan had a companion who read to her each afternoon. But the companion had gone away for a week's holiday before Christmas. Had Mrs Sullivan got anyone to read to her for that week?

"I read quite well," thought Betsy. "I'm the very best in my class. I even read all the hard words without being bothered by them. I shall go tomorrow and ask Mrs Sullivan if she would like me to read to her. Then, if she pays me, I shall be doing my bit, too."

She didn't tell the others in case they laughed at her. But next morning after breakfast she went down the snowy street and found Mrs Sullivan's house.

The snow was now very thick. It had snowed all night long and in places it was as high as Betsy's knees. She liked it. It was fun to

clamber through the soft white snow. She knocked at Mrs Sullivan's door.

She felt a bit frightened. Mrs Sullivan was rather a fierce-looking old lady and she wore dark glasses that made her look fiercer still. Suppose she was cross that Betsy should dare to come and ask to read to her?

Then Betsy thought of her mother's lost purse with all the money in it. This was one small way of helping. She couldn't turn back now!

Mrs Sullivan's daily woman opened the door and took Betsy into a little room where a bright fire burned. A big cat sat beside the old lady. The radio was on, and music flooded the little room. When Betsy spoke, Mrs Sullivan put out her hand, and turned the radio off.

"Well, it's little Betsy Jameson, is it?" she said. "And what do you want, Betsy?"

"Mrs Sullivan, I heard that your companion is away for a week's holiday," said Betsy, "and I didn't know if you'd got anyone to read to you in the afternoons. You see, Mummy has lost her purse with all her Christmas money in it, and we're trying to earn a bit to make up – so I thought . . ."

"You thought I might pay you for reading to

me, did you?" said Mrs Sullivan. "Well, I shall have to try you. There's a book somewhere – pick it up and read me a page."

Betsy found the library book. She began to read in her clear little voice. Mrs Sullivan listened with a smile on her face.

"Yes, you read quite well for your age – ten, aren't you? I shall be pleased to engage you. I will pay you a pound an hour for reading to me. Come at two o'clock each afternoon, starting today."

Betsy felt very proud – but a pound an hour seemed a lot of money just for reading. "I'd come for fifty pence really," she said. "I'm not as good as a grown-up at reading."

"I shall love to have you," said Mrs Sullivan. "You won't mind if we don't have reading all the time, will you? I mean, it would be nice to talk sometimes, wouldn't it?"

"Oh yes. But you wouldn't want to pay me just for talking," said Betsy.

"Well, I'll pay you for your time," said Mrs Sullivan. "Whether it's reading or talking, or just stroking my cat for me, I'll pay you for keeping me company."

"Thank you very much," said Betsy, and she stood up. "I'll come at two o'clock. I won't be late."

She went home as fast as she could through the snow. She had something to tell the others! A whole pound an hour for six days. If Mrs Sullivan kept her for two hours each afternoon, that would be twelve pounds altogether – more than enough to buy a chicken, surely!

Robert and Ellen thought it was marvellous. They had news to tell, too. "I've got the job at the butcher's," said Robert. "He asked me a few questions, and rang up my headmaster, and then said I could come till the other boy is well. I've got to deliver orders from ten to twelve o'clock each morning, and from three to five each afternoon. And he'll give me extra money on Saturdays."

"Oh, good!" said Ellen. "Considering you're only thirteen, you're jolly lucky to get a job as easily as that. You'll have to be careful not to mix up any of the orders."

"Of course I shall," said Robert, rather indignantly. "How did you get on with your job, Ellen?"

"Well, Mrs Harris was very pleased," said Ellen. "She's going to pay me five pounds each afternoon for taking all the children out. They're thrilled! I like little children, so I shall enjoy it. Between us we shall get quite a bit of money for Mummy."

"How much is Robert earning?" said Betsy.

"Five pounds a day," said Robert, "and the butcher will let me have meat at a cheaper price. Not bad considering it's only a few hours a day. By Christmas we'll have loads of money – enough for everything we need for a Christmas feast."

"And perhaps a little Christmas tree," Betsy said hopefully.

The next thing to be done was to tell Mother

what they had arranged. How they hoped she wouldn't say they mustn't. Mother listened without a word. Then she spoke in rather a shaky voice.

"Yes, you can all do your little jobs, bless you. I don't think I mind losing my purse when I know what nice children I've got. I'm proud of you all. The money will certainly help to buy the things we need."

Nobody brought Mrs Jameson's purse back to her. Robert thought that people must be very mean indeed not to take a purse back to the person who lost it. He called at the police station twice to ask if anyone had brought it in. But nobody had.

All the children began their jobs that day. Robert went off to the butcher's, and listened attentively when Mr Hughes told him about the deliveries. "The addresses are on the labels of each order," he said. "Be sure to deliver at the right house, and whatever you do, don't leave anything on the doorstep in order to be quick. If there is no one home bring it back to the shop."

Robert set off with a basket filled with orders for meat and poultry. The snow was very thick indeed, and it was a long job taking all the orders round. Everyone was very

surprised to see him, but when he told them why he was doing it they all smiled and nodded.

"It's a pity more children don't do things like that," said Mr George. "Helping their mothers when things go wrong."

Ellen got on very well too. The three small Harris children were delighted to see her. John, Mike and Sally all tried to cling to her hand at once. She set off very happily with them through the deep, white snow.

"We'll play snowballing. We'll build a snowman in the park and I'll try and build you a little snow-house," promised Ellen. They all had a lovely time, and when she brought them back to their mother at teatime Mrs Harris exclaimed in delight at their rosy faces and happy talk.

"Oh, Ellen, you've given them such a nice time. Here is your money. You'll come again tomorrow, won't you? The children will so look forward to it."

"I feel sorry you've got to pay me for my afternoon," said Ellen, feeling quite ashamed of taking the money. "I've had just as good a time as the children, Mrs Harris. I really have."

"Just wait a minute – I've been baking while

you've been out," said Mrs Harris. "I've got a
cake for you to take home for yourself and
that brother and sister of yours – what are
their names – Robert and Betsy?"

And she gave Ellen a lovely chocolate cake,
wrapped up in paper. Ellen was delighted.
How surprised Robert and Betsy would be!
She thanked Mrs Harris and hurried off home.

She met Betsy at the gate. Betsy's cheeks were red from Mrs Sullivan's bright fire, and from stumbling home through the thick snow. "Look," she said, showing Ellen her two bright coins. "That's my first wage. And isn't it lovely, Ellen, Mrs Sullivan likes just the kind of stories I like. We read a most exciting school story for a whole hour!"

Mother smiled at all the cheerful talk. She had made hot toast and butter with honey and the chocolate cake was put in a place of honour on the table. The children sat down hungrily.

"And Mrs Sullivan and I talked a lot," said Betsy. "She told me all about when she was a girl – oh, ever so long ago – and I told her about Robert and Ellen and you, Mummy. And then I had to brush the cat, Jimmy, and get him some milk. I really did have a very nice time. I can hardly wait till tomorrow to find out what happens in the story I'm reading to Mrs Sullivan."

"I bet she chose a story like that because you wouldn't be able to read a grown up one," said Robert.

"She didn't! She laughed at all the funny bits too," said Betsy. "There's a Mamselle in the book and the girls are always playing tricks on her. We laughed like anything."

"Mrs Sullivan is very kind," said Mother. "Very, very kind. I ought to pay her for having you like this."

"Oh no, Mummy – it's a job of work, really it is," said Betsy, earnestly. "Mrs Sullivan says it's not easy to be a really good companion, and she says I am. Really she does."

"You're a lovely little companion," said Mother. "Mrs Sullivan is lucky to have you. But I think she knows it. Well, as I have said before – what nice children I have got!"

"Well, we've got a jolly nice mother," said Robert, unexpectedly. "And what's more, Mum, I once heard the headmaster's wife saying to the head that she had noticed that all the nicest children were the ones that had the best mothers – so, if you think we're nice, you've got yourself to thank!"

Everybody laughed. They all felt happy and cosy. It was so nice to help and to do a job well. Really it didn't seem to matter any more that Mrs Jameson had lost her purse.

All the children went to their jobs each day, cheerfully and willingly. Mr Hughes the butcher, Mrs Harris, and blind Mrs Sullivan welcomed them and wished there were more children like them. Robert didn't deliver any

345

wrong orders, Ellen made the three Harris children happy, and as for Betsy, it would be hard to know which of the two, she or Mrs Sullivan, enjoyed themselves the more.

"Jimmy always purrs loudly when he sees me coming," Betsy said. "I wish I had a kitten. Jimmy purrs like a boiling kettle. It's a pity Mrs Sullivan can't see how nice he looks when I've brushed him."

By the time that the day before Christmas came the children had given their mother quite a lot of money. Enough to buy the chicken, the fruit and a box of crackers. Marvellous!

Just as Robert was going home on Christmas Eve morning for his lunch, Mrs Toms called him. She lived in a little house in the middle of the village and she was a friend of his mother's.

"Robert! Would you have time to sweep away the snow for me before you go to the butcher's this afternoon? I did ask a man to come and do it but he hasn't turned up, and I've got my sister and her children coming for Christmas Day tomorrow. I know you're earning money for your mother and I'd be very glad to pay you for the sweeping."

"No, I'll do it for nothing," said Robert. "I'd like to. It would be nice to do something for nothing for a change, Mrs Toms. Have you got a broom and a spade? If you have I'll come along at two o'clock this afternoon, before I go to Mr Hughes, and clean up your front path for you."

"You're a kind child," said Mrs Toms. "Thank you very much. If you won't let me pay you I shall give you some of our apples and pears for Christmas instead. I had a lot from my garden this year and I've saved plenty. So you shall have a basket to take home."

Christmas was going to be good after all, thought Robert as he went home. He was out again just before two and went to Mrs Toms's house. The spade and broom were waiting for him outside the front door. Robert took the spade first. How thick and deep the snow was! Except for a little path, it had been untouched for days and was quite deep.

He began to dig, shovelling the snow away to the side. He worked hard, and soon took off his coat, he felt so hot.

When he got almost up to the front door he dug his spade into the snow, and threw aside a great heap. As the snow fell, something dark showed in it. It tumbled to the side with the snow. Robert glanced at it.

Then he looked again, more carefully. He dropped his spade and picked it up. It was a brown purse!

"Mrs Toms! I've found Mum's purse!" yelled Robert, suddenly, making Mrs Toms almost jump out of her skin. "Look, it's buried in the snow outside your front door."

Mrs Toms came hurrying out. "My goodness, is it really her purse? Yes, it is. She must have dropped it in the snow when she came

delivering the parish magazines some days ago. Would you believe it! And now you've found it! Well, well – what a good thing you're a kind-hearted lad and came to sweep the snow away for me – or someone else might have found it and taken it, when the snow melted."

"I'll just finish this," Robert said, joyfully, "then maybe I'll have time to rush home and tell Mum before I start at the butcher's. Oh, aren't I lucky. I can hardly believe it!"

He rushed home with the purse. Ellen and Betsy were not there; they had gone to their jobs. But Mother was there, and she stared in delight when Robert held out the wet purse.

"Robert! Oh, Robert, where did you find it? Is my money in it? Oh yes, everything's there, quite safe. Oh, Robert, this is wonderful. Just in time for Christmas, too! I shall go shopping this very afternoon, because now I shall be able to buy you all the presents I thought you would have to go without. It's too good to be true!"

It was a very happy and joyful Christmas for the Jameson family that year. There was plenty to eat after all, and as much fruit and chocolate and sweets as anyone wanted. There was a Christmas tree hung with all kinds of

things and topped with a lovely Father
Christmas which Mrs Sullivan gave to Betsy.
Mrs Toms sent a basket of apples and pears.
Mrs Harris gave Ellen a big box of chocolates
for everyone. And Mr Hughes presented Robert
with a big fat turkey and a pound of sausages.

"Everybody's so kind," said Ellen, happily.
"Oh, Mummy – these are wonderful paints
you've given me."

"And my model aeroplane kit is much better than I expected," said Robert. "Mum, you've bought me a more expensive one than I said – it'll make a much bigger aeroplane."

"I shall call my doll Angela Rosemary Caroline Jameson," said Betsy, hugging an enormous doll. "She's the biggest doll I've ever seen and the nicest. Oh, Mummy – we never thought Christmas would be like this, did we, when you lost your purse?"

"No," said Mrs Jameson, who was busy putting all her things from her old handbag into her new red one. "We didn't. I didn't think I'd have this lovely bag, for instance. I didn't think I'd be able to get all the things you wanted, or any nice things to eat. But you've managed it between you. I'm proud of you. There aren't many children who would do what you have done."

Isn't it marvellous how a bit of bad luck can be changed into something good if everybody helps!